MAFIA DADDY
A Dark Mafia Romance
By
Abby Slash

Dedicated to My Leo My Ari and for you reading my story I am grateful! Thank You

Copyright © 2025 by Abby Slash

All rights reserved.

No part of this book may be reproduced in any form or by any electronic or mechanical means, including information storage and retrieval systems, without written permission from the author, except for the use of brief quotations in a book review.

Dedicated to you thanks for reading my debut Dark Mafia Novel! Grateful. To my Leo for believing in me!

Preface
Sound Track
Scent of a woman
Hallelujah
Me and the Devil

Chapter 1

Ivy

"I must survive, it's the only option I have!"

Oh God I must do this! Voices in my head ran rampant. I trembled. Anxiety getting the best of me! What did I sign up for? I closed my eyes but it did no good.

"Hiss!" The sound jolted me back to reality.

The train hissed to a final stop, its doors groaning open like a tired exhale.

I sighed.

I tightened my grip around the worn strap of my duffel bag, and stepped down onto the platform alone.

The familiar scent of the city was there, exhaust, rain-soaked pavement, but it was laced now with a sense of danger, undetected yet palpable.

I shot a quick glance over my shoulder, searching for any sign of pursuit. Nothing. But that didn't mean I wasn't being watched.

With each step, the city's chill seeped through the soles of my boots, a cold reminder that this place, once a playground of childhood memories, had turned into a battlefield of shadows and deceptions.

I hugged my coat tighter around my curves, as if the thin fabric could shield me from the sinister gaze I felt prickling at the back of my neck.

The walk to the estate was a blur of grays and browns, the sky a canvas of gloom overhead. When the iron gates loomed before me, two men materialized out of the mist, their postures rigid, the glint of gunmetal betraying their purpose.

They eyed me with the kind of suspicion reserved for strangers or enemies.

"Can I help you?" one growled, a hint of threat woven through his words.

I stood firm, steeling myself against the rush of memories that threatened to weaken my resolve. "I need to see Dominic Mancini," I stated, my voice firmer than I felt. The weight of my father's name hung in the air between us, a talisman and a curse.

For a moment, their expressions flickered with recognition, then shuttered closed once more. They exchanged a look, a silent conversation passing between them before they stepped aside. I didn't wait for an invitation; I walked past them, my heart pounding an unfamiliar rhythm against my ribs.

As the grandeur of the estate felt massive. Here I was, teetering on the precipice of sanctuary and ruin, invoking the name of a man who owed me nothing but a promise made long ago. A worthy promise

* * *

"Dominic Mancini? The Boss?"

The name slipped from the guard's lips like a whisper of the past, and I could feel the tremor in the air before I saw him. The large oak doors at the far end of the foyer creaked open, and for a moment, time seemed to hesitate on the brink of something inevitable.

He emerged from the shadows that clung to the mansion's opulent interior, the dim light casting his figure in sharp relief.

Dominic Mancini.

The man who had become myth in my mind since I last saw him, the silent guardian my father once spoke of in reverent tones.

Even so I freaking fantasized about him taking me often! Driving his massive thickness into my virgin slit! Stop it Ivy this is a matter of life and death and remember he's dangerous too! Or at least that is what the myth about him said!

His stride was purposeful, commanding, as if the very ground he walked on dared not question his authority. I watched him approach, each step bringing back the memories of a girl who used to look up to him, of whispered promises and fierce protectiveness.

But the years had stretched between us, filled with ghosts and sins neither of us could escape. He halted before me, his presence overwhelming, and our eyes locked, a collision of past and present. I searched for traces of the man I remembered, but found only the hardened lines of power and ruthlessness etched into his face.

"Dominic," I said, my voice steadier than my quivering heart.

His gaze swept over me, taking in the changes wrought by time. The young nineteen year old he knew was gone, replaced by someone who bore the marks of a life that had demanded too much, too soon. I felt his assessment, a wordless judgment that left me feeling exposed.

"Leave," he said, his voice a low command that brooked no argument.

But I stood my ground, summoning every ounce of defiance I possessed. "I can't," I replied, meeting his challenge. I looked up, driven by desperation and the knowledge that there was nowhere left for me to run.

There was a beat of silence, a crackling tension that filled the space between us. In his eyes, I saw the war that raged within him, the duty he owed to his own name and the promise made to a man who had been more than just an ally.

"Please," I added, softer now. It was not a word I used lightly, but the gravity of my situation left me no room for pride.

Dominic clenched his jaw, the muscle ticking with silent fury. He studied me with a critical eye, weighing his options, calculating the risk I posed. And though the word hung unspoken in the air, I knew what this decision would cost him.

"Fine," he finally spat out, the word tasting of reluctance and resentment. But it was enough, and a shiver of relief ran through me.

For now, this was my reprieve, my harbor in the storm. Tomorrow's consequences lingered on the horizon, but tonight, I was safe, or as safe as one could be under the roof of a man like Dominic Mancini.

* * *

I braced myself against the chill of the evening and the colder reception before me. Dominic's gaze was a fortress wall, his stance unyielding as he towered in the doorway.

"You don't understand," I said, my voice steadier than I felt. "I'm running from Matteo. He's... he's not who I thought he was." My fingers twitched around the strap of my duffel bag, seeking something solid to hold onto. "He's being groomed to take over the northern sector for his family."

A flicker of recognition, or perhaps concern? passed through Dominic's eyes.

The mention of rival territory was enough to stir the air of danger that always cloaked him. Still, his expression remained a mask of indifference, his voice low and controlled.

"Matteo DeMarco?" His name was a curse on Dominic's lips, a testament to feuds that ran as deep as bloodlines.

"Yes," I whispered, the truth pressing down on me like the weight of the life I was trying to escape. "You promised my dad you'd protect me." The words were a key, turning in the lock of an oath made long ago.

Dominic sighed, then he remained silent.

Dominic's silence stretched out, taut as the string of a violin waiting for a maestro's touch. Finally, with a curt nod, he stepped aside. "One night, Ivy," he conceded, each word measured and heavy with unspoken terms. "One night only."

I nodded, swallowing the lump of gratitude and fear in my throat.

There were no thanks to offer that could bridge the gulf between us, no pleas that would lighten the burden I'd just placed on his shoulders.

"Understand this," Dominic continued, his voice a steel edge wrapped in velvet. "There are no illusions here. No expectations." His cold hazel eyes bore into mine, demanding acknowledgment, submission to the rules he set within his world.

"Understood," I replied, my voice barely above a whisper. It was all I could promise when my very presence spelled potential chaos for both our lives.

* * *

The door to the room swung open with a silent, ominous grace that contradicted the violence simmering just beneath the surface of Dominic Mancini's estate. The guard who escorted me gestured inside without a word, his eyes never quite meeting mine. I stepped over the threshold, the weight of my duffel bag somehow grounding me in the unreality of it all.

I was alone when the door clicked shut behind me, sealing me into a chamber too grand for the likes of me. Gold-leafed frames boasted renaissance art on walls that soared to a frescoed ceiling, mocking me with their opulence. A king-sized bed dressed in silken linens looked cold and uninviting despite its finery. The room was a cage gilded in luxury, beautiful yet imprisoning.

I dropped my bag and walked to the window, peering between heavy velvet drapes at the darkening grounds below. The view offered manicured lawns fading into shadows, but I might as well have been staring at a brick wall for all the freedom it promised. My reflection in the glass stared back at me, a girl out of her depth in a world that demanded more than she could give.

I turned away from my own haunted eyes and sank onto the edge of the bed, the whisper of the sheets like a sigh in the silence. This was the safest place for me, here in the lion's den, where the beast prowled just out of sight. And yet, it was also the most dangerous place I'd ever been. In seeking refuge, I had stepped into the eye of a storm that freaking raged between our families for years.

My gaze drifted to the door, solid and unyielding. It was a barrier and a protection, a reminder of the promise made by a man who now seemed a stranger. This fortress was my sanctuary for one night only, an ephemeral respite from the chase. But even in this stillness, I knew I was not alone.

Somewhere beyond these walls, I imagined Dominic's eyes on me, those icy gorgeous eyes that saw through pretense and fear. I pictured him in some dimly lit room, surrounded by screens that laid bare the secrets of his domain.

"Dominic," I murmured to the empty room, letting his sexy name hang in the air, a talisman against the darkness creeping into my heart.

Cutting through the quiet of my solitude came a different kind of silence—the sense that someone watched, listened, waited. It wrapped around me, a tangible presence that prickled at my skin.

"Damn it, Ivy," his voice would be a muted growl, barely audible over the hum of electronics and the distant sounds of the city outside the high walls. "What the hell are you doing here?"

But Dominic Mancini wasn't the kind of man to ask questions he didn't already know the answers to. He was the kind of man who watched, always watching from his fortress, calculating each move in a game that I had just stumbled back into.

I closed my eyes, leaning back against the mountain of pillows, a princess in a tower of her own making. But unlike the fairy tales, there was no prince coming to rescue me. There was only the night, the silence, and the dangerous comfort of a promise made in blood.

Chapter 2
Ivy

I woke to the luxurious silk's kiss against my skin, a strange luxury juxtaposed with the dull ache that pulsed in my body.

My mind, still groggy from sleep and the shadows of nightmare, flitted back to the bruises I had fought so hard to escape.

In the semi-darkness of the opulent room, my gaze fixed on the unblinking eye of a security camera perched high in the corner. Shivers ran down my spine as I clutched the blanket tighter around me, the fabric failing to shield me from the chill of being constantly watched.

"Damn Dominic," I whispered under my breath. years of having a deep crush now feels like a weight over my entire being! I wondered what he was doing or thinking at the moment?

Dominic

Downstairs, the mansion hummed with the silent weight of secrets and power. I sat in my study, surrounded by the scent of leather and aged paper. The heavy wooden furniture, the shelves crammed with ancient books, all of it cast a familiar shadow across my world. Old-world authority. That's what they said about me. Maybe it was true. But tonight, I felt anything but in control.

The screen in front of me glowed with pale light, illuminating her. Her.

The restless figure from moments earlier, pacing like a caged animal in the room I had reluctantly given her. She looked like she wanted to burn the walls down with her fury. And still, I couldn't look away.

One of my men leaned over my shoulder, his eyes locked on the monitor.

"Boss, you weren't kidding when you said she's gorgeous," he said, his voice tainted with something filthy.

I clenched my jaw. I didn't need to look at him. I didn't need to raise my voice. Just let the steel slip into my tone. "Eyes on the job, not on the girl," I snapped, my words cutting through the air.

He stepped back right away. Smart move.

But even as silence returned, something inside me twisted. My fingers hovered, still against the polished wood of the desk. That comment shouldn't have mattered. It shouldn't have touched anything real. But it did. Because she wasn't just any girl.

And that was the problem.

A crack had formed in the mask I wore every day. The cold, calculated calm I had spent years perfecting faltered for just a moment. There were lines I never crossed. Walls I had built to keep certain things locked away. But every second I watched her, every breath she took behind that door upstairs, those lines started to fade.

And I wasn't sure how much longer I could keep them intact.

***

Ivy

The aroma of fresh coffee and baked bread wafted through the expansive kitchen as I made my entrance, the soft silk of Dominic's shirt grazing my thighs with every step. It hung loosely on my frame, an impromptu garment that felt like a whispered secret against my skin. The morning light spilled in through the grand windows, casting a golden glow that seemed at odds with the tension that hung in the air, thick and unspoken.

Dominic sat at the head of the table, a king in his domestic domain, the newspaper unfolded before him like a barrier. He looked up as I approached, and for a moment too long, his dark eyes lingered on me, tracing the contours of the shirt that was all I wore. I caught the flicker of something, perhaps a ghost of a storm before he regained his composure. I smirked, challenging the silence between us. "Didn't think you'd mind."

His gaze snapped back to the newspaper, but the damage was done. There was a crack in his armor, microscopic perhaps, but it was there. I poured myself a cup of coffee, the steam curling into the air like a sinful promise. My voice was light but laced with daring as I leaned against the marble counter. "Do I still look like my father's little daughter to you?"

The question hung in the air, a provocation wrapped in innocence. Dominic didn't answer, his jaw tightening, the lines of his face hardening into a mask of control. But his silence was a intense, screaming the unsaid words we both knew hovered on the edge of his restraint.

I sipped my coffee, the bitter taste grounding me as I watched him. There was power in this game, a dangerous dance on the precipice of something neither of us could afford to fall into. And yet, here we were, teetering on the brink.

The morning light spilled over the marble countertop, casting long shadows across the kitchen floor. I moved around the space with ease now, familiar with its grandeur and cold beauty. I reached for a glass in the overhead cabinet, the hem of Dominic's shirt riding up my thighs. As I bent over the counter to fill it, my backside brushed against something solid. I bit my lower lip to stifle a moan, could it be? Would it fit? Oh God Ivy get it together!

Behind me was the only sound that broke the stillness.

I straightened slowly, turning my head just enough to catch the reflection in the window. Dominic stood there, his body rigid, his hands white-knuckled as they clung to the edge of the marble. The veins in his arms stood out, a network of tension and barely restrained power. My heart thumped erratically, both thrilled and terrified at the proximity.

"Dominic?" I said, my voice feigning innocence while my eyes told a different story. They were dark with unspoken promises and challenges, daring him to cross the line he had so firmly drawn.

His smirked, the muscles ticking as he fought for control. And then, as if compelled by some unseen force, he turned away from me, his gaze fixed on the abstract painting that adorned the far wall. It didn't fool me; I knew he was watching me, always watching, with those intense eyes that seemed to strip away all my defenses.

I leaned back against the counter, tilting my head to one side as I played with the edge of the oversized shirt. "You know, my ex used to say that no one would ever want me untouched and still a virgin," I mused aloud, my tone light but laced with venom for the man who no longer held any claim over me.

The moment the words left my lips, the air in the room shifted, crackling with a dangerous energy. Dominic spun around, his expression dark and furious. "He's wrong," he growled, the words slicing through the tension like a knife. They came out too quickly, too raw, betraying a passion that Dominic rarely allowed himself to show.

I felt thrilling sensations running through me, a wild satisfaction at having provoked such a response. His anger wasn't directed at me, it was protective, possessive even. It was a slip, a crack in his stoic façade, and I reveled in it.

"Is that so?" I whispered, stepping closer to him, feeling the heat that radiated from his body. My pulse hammered in my ears, and I could see the same fire reflected back at me in his eyes. We were playing with fire, dancing along the edge of a precipice that threatened to consume us both.

And yet, I couldn't stop.

* * *

My heart thumped fast as I leaned into him. The air between us was thick with unspoken promises and dangerous intentions. "Then take me," I whispered, my voice a siren's call that pulled at the tethers of his restraint.

In an instant, Dominic slammed his hands against the wall, just inches from my face. His toned body against mine, his eyes a stormy sea threatening to drown us both. We were so close I could feel the heat of his breath mingling with mine, each exhale a silent plea for something we both knew we couldn't have. His lips hovered near, so near I could almost taste the bitter tang of longing for them to crush onto mine.

Holy freaking heck—

My intimate walls clenched hard with need.

But then, without a word, he stepped away, leaving me in the wake of what could have been.

The silence that followed was deafening. My breath came out in ragged gasps, a testament to the chaos he'd stirred within me. I touched the wall where his hand had been, half expecting it to be as hot as the fire in his gaze.

* * *

Later, I found Dominic in his private gym, the sanctuary where he unleashed his demons. He was punishing the punching bag, his fists relentless and unforgiving. Blood trickled from his knuckles, painting a stark contrast on the white wraps that bound them. Each thud against the leather echoed like a confession.

"She's a fucking angel," he muttered between strikes, his voice low and laced with a torment that clenched my heart. The words vibrated through the room, heavy with a truth he refused to acknowledge anywhere but here, in the solitude of his pain.

"He'll kill me." The last part was barely audible over the sound of leather colliding with flesh and bone. Yet it carried the weight of a thousand sins, of loyalty and duty that shackled him to a path he had never chosen.

I stood there, unseen, watching the man who had men in his home fall apart under the burden of his own heart. And in that moment, I realized that the line that separated us, captor and captive, guardian and ward began to blur.

Chapter 3

Ivy

I flipped the page of the ancient mafia history tome, the crisp sound reverberating off the high walls of the library.

I skimmed over the bolded names of crime lords long dead, but I wasn't reading, not really. Every so often, my gaze lifted to catch Dominic's steely gaze, a silent game of provocation played out in the space between us.

His posture was rigid, a sentinel guarding secrets and sorrow. With each stare, I felt him like a storm on the horizon, a tempest trapped in the body of a man who had seen too much. The air around us was charged with an electricity that seemed to hum with the weight of unspoken words.

"Dammit, Ivy." His voice was a low growl as he turned away, the muscles in his jaw working overtime. "I can't babysit you all day."

"Who's asking you to?" My reply was nonchalant, a mask of indifference while my heart raced beneath the surface.

Dominic paced to the other end of the room, picking up a phone with a purpose that suggested retreat. He spoke tersely into the receiver, his back to me now, a barrier erected to shield himself from whatever it was about me that seemed to unravel him.

"Marco, I need you upstairs," he commanded, his tone brokering no argument. Dominic was done playing games; boundaries were being set. But lines on the ground did little to contain the wildfire that was slowly kindling between us.

With a final glance that held a warning sharp enough to cut glass, Dominic stepped out of the room, leaving behind a silence that pounded louder than any words. Now there would be another set of eyes on me, another member of Dominic's world to watch as I moved through this gilded cage.

But as the door clicked shut behind him, I couldn't help but feel a twinge of victory. For all his power, for all his command, Dominic was retreating, and I, Ivy, the girl he was forced to watch over, had driven him to it.

* * *

The door to the library creaked, a telltale sign of Marco's return. I eyed him over the top of my book, a leather-bound tome heavy with mafia lore, a prop in our little game of cat and mouse. His eyes avoided mine, skittering away like pebbles kicked across the floor.

"Speak," I commanded, adopting a tone that mimicked Dominic's own authoritative timbre. It was a façade, for I had no real power here, but this small act of defiance lent me a sense of control.

"Miss Ivy," Marco began, his voice low and laced with unease, "you keep asking about things that ain't good for your health." He shifted from foot to foot, the messenger bearing unwanted tidings. "Questions about Mr. Mancini's past, his enemies, scars..."

"Is that forbidden?" My words were a challenge wrapped in innocence.

Marco just shook his head, a silent plea for me to understand unspoken rules. But I didn't want to understand; I wanted to unravel the enigma that was Dominic Mancini.

Later that evening, the tension in the air was thick enough to choke on as Dominic stormed into the library. The faint scent of aged leather and lingering cologne trailed behind him like the remnants of a storm. His dark eyes were thunderclouds, promising destruction.

"Have you lost your mind?" he growled, frustration sharpening each syllable. "Questioning my men about my life?"

I stood up slowly, closing the distance between us with a few measured steps. My heart hammered against my chest, a drumbeat of exhilaration and fear. "Are you afraid of me, Dominic? Or are you afraid of what you'll do to me?"

His jaw clenched visibly, muscles working beneath the stubble-shaded skin. The air shifted, crackling with something dangerous, a mix of anger and desire that neither of us could name.

"Your curiosity will hurt you, Ivy," he warned, voice laden with threats and an undercurrent of something else, concern, maybe?

"Then stop me," I whispered, tilting my head back to meet his gaze. The challenge hung between us, an invitation and a dare all at once.

Dominic exhaled heavily, betraying the ironclad composure he wore like armor. For a moment, I thought he might close the gap, shatter the fragile truce we danced around day after day. But instead, he stepped back, the lines of his shoulders rigid with restraint.

"Be careful, Ivy," he said, the words rough like gravel. "Not everything you're curious about is worth knowing."

And then he turned and left, leaving me alone with the echo of his warning and the knowledge that despite the walls he tried to erect, I had gotten under his skin.

***

Dominic

As I prowled the shadow-draped corridors of my sprawling estate, the soft glow from Ivy's room caught my eye.

The door was ajar, just enough to hint at an invitation or perhaps a careless mistake. Indecision gripped me for a heartbeat, but the memory of her challenge pulsed through my mind, a siren call I refused to answer.

I stood there, my gaze locked on that sliver of light, every muscle in my body tensed to move, but I remained rooted in place. With a silent curse, I turned away from the possibility of what lay beyond that door.

Retreating to the solace of my study, I poured myself a glass of aged whiskey, its amber liquid mirroring the turmoil swirling within me. Each sip burned down my throat, a futile attempt to scorch away the images flooding my thoughts.

Ivy, with her defiant eyes and incessant questions, had become a tempest I couldn't control. I ran a hand over my face, feeling the weight of years and sins etched into my skin.

I sank into the leather chair, the familiar scent grounding me as the whiskey left a trail of fire in its wake. My mind wandered back to the promise made to her father, a vow soaked in blood and sealed with the heavy burden of protection. Back then, she was nothing more than a child with wide, innocent eyes and a laugh that echoed through these halls. Now, she was all sharp edges and smoldering glances, her adult form a haunting silhouette against the backdrop of my darkened life.

My jaw clenched involuntarily, the memories a jarring juxtaposition. She'd grown up under my watch, a flower blooming in a bed of thorns. And I, caught between the man I was and the protector I had sworn to be, was losing ground to the forbidden thoughts that threatened to overtake me. With each passing day, the line I dared not cross became more blurred.

The echoing silence of the room wrapped around me like a shroud as the last drops of whiskey clung to the crystal. I should have felt comfort in the solitude, yet it was her presence, so near yet out of reach, that filled the space, leaving me restless and uncertain. I set the glass down with a quiet thud, the sound a grave note in the symphony of my inner turmoil.

In the end, I chose duty over desire, the shadows my only companions as I wrestled with the ghosts of past and present. But even as I surrendered to the night, a part of me remained vigilant, listening for the faintest whisper of movement from the room with the door left slightly open.

***

Ivy

I turned a corner in the dimly lit corridor and stumbled upon him like a secret just waiting to be discovered. There he was, Dominic, shirtless amidst the shadows, his skin pale against the darkness, working on bandaging a wound that marred his otherwise unyielding form. The white gauze stark against his olive skin, wrapped tightly around his torso, spoke of violence I could only guess at.

The sight stole my breath. I had seen many things in this house, but never Dominic, the ever-composed Don, so raw and exposed. He didn't startle or cover himself; those ice-hazel eyes simply met mine, as if he'd been expecting me all along.

"Go to bed, Ivy," he said, his voice rough yet controlled, threading through the silence between us.

I stepped closer before he could say another word.

His scars, a map of his brutal legacy, pulled me in, and I reached out, my fingertips grazing the raised, harsh line across his ribs. There was a story there, one of pain and survival.

"Make me," I whispered back, the words escaping me, laced with an audacity I hadn't known I possessed.

For a moment, he was still, his breathing shallow, the tension in the room winding tighter like a coiled spring. Then he turned away, the muscles in his back rippling under the faint light, his movements deliberate as he resumed the task of covering up the evidence of his life's work.

But as he walked past me, he placed his hand on my shoulder, and it lingered there longer than necessary, longer than he'd ever allowed himself before. The warmth of his touch seared through the fabric of my top, branding me with a yearning I wasn't sure either of us understood.

"Goodnight, Ivy," he murmured, his voice betraying a hint of something unnamed before he pulled away, leaving me alone with the ghost of his touch and the echo of a connection we were both terrified to acknowledge.

Chapter 4

Dominic

The phone's buzzing sound sliced through the silence of my study like a warning shot. I knew before I picked up who it would be, and why. Still, my heart hammered as I answered, the cool veneer I wore daily thinning with each pulse.

"Dominic," came his gruff voice, a sound worn by time and command. "We need to talk."

I straightened in my chair, the leather creaking under me. "I'll be there in twenty."

The drive to Don Tano's estate was short, but my thoughts stretched and tangled like shadows at dusk. I rehearsed lines in my head, planning my report, carefully curating what to share—and what to bury deep beneath layers of half-truths.

In his office, a room that reeked of power and aged scotch, he waited. His eyes, always so piercing, searched mine for signs of deceit. I met his gaze evenly, the perfect picture of loyalty.

"Dominic," he began, his tone heavy with concern, "the tensions are rising. The Sartori family is making moves; we can't afford any surprises."

"Understood," I said, my voice steady as the oak desk between us. "I've got my men on it. We won't be caught off guard."

"Good." He leaned back, the leather chair groaning in protest. "You know you're the only one I trust with this, right?"

"Of course, Don Tano," I replied, pushing down the twinge of guilt that came uninvited.

As I left his office, the weight of his trust settled on my shoulders, a mantle I bore with increasing unease. I made my way quietly back home, where secrets were the currency, and my biggest one moved within the walls with grace and trepidation.

Back in the sanctuary of my domain, I noticed the door to the library slightly ajar. A sliver of light spilled out onto the darkened hallway floor. I approached silently, my instincts honed from years in the shadows serving me well. As I neared, the muffled sounds of voices reached my ears, and I paused.

"…still considers Dominic his most trusted ally."

It was Ivy's voice, a whisper tainted with sorrow. She had been listening, I realized, an accidental eavesdropper caught by the gravity of her father's words. Her presence there, an unexpected witness to our conversation, twisted inside me.

I lingered by the door, unseen. Her guilt radiated like heat from a flame, and I could almost feel its burn. For a moment, I shared in it, the duplicity of our situation seeping into the marrow of my bones. But then I moved on, leaving her with the echo of her father's misplaced faith.

That night, the mansion lay quiet, but the ghosts of our choices haunted the halls, whispering of the lines we'd crossed and those still ahead, waiting.

* * *

Silence ruled the house like a solemn king, its reign unchallenged until the faint strains of music trickled through the emptiness. I followed the sound, threading through shadows that clung to my footsteps, until I reached the living room. There, amidst the opulence that spoke of power and danger, was Ivy. Her feet were bare against the cold marble floor, her movements fluid as she danced alone, lost in the soft melody that seemed out of place in a world as hardened as ours.

The sight of her, so carefree and wrapped in an aura of innocence, was a stark contrast to the day's tension-filled meetings and whispered threats. It was lethal, this purity of hers, slicing through defenses I didn't realize I had erected. I leaned against the darkened doorway, the predator within lulled into stillness by the grace of the unsuspecting swan.

"Dominic?" Her voice cut through the music as she turned and caught sight of me. She didn't stop dancing, though. "I didn't hear you come in."

I clenched my jaw, every instinct telling me this charade couldn't continue. "It has to stop," I said, my voice barely above the haunting piano notes filling the space between us.

Her dance slowed, then stilled entirely, and she approached me with a gaze that held too much knowing for someone her age. She stepped into my space without hesitation, a defiance that matched the bloodline she carried. Her hand found its way to my chest, the warmth of her skin burning through the fabric of my shirt.

"Then why haven't you stopped it?" she asked, tilting her head up to meet my eyes, searching for something I wasn't sure I could give. I got so hard I had to adjust my bulge in that moment discreetly why was she doing this?

In that moment, the weight of our reality pressed down on me, heavy as the silence that returned when the song ended.

I couldn't help it dammit Ivy why do you do this to me?

I crushed my lips to hers, the need that had been simmering beneath the surface for too long. Her response was immediate and fierce, her hands tangling in my hair as if she were fighting to keep me anchored to this precipice we teetered on. Our lips moved as one with a hunger born from the forbidden, each kiss a defiance against the rules that bound us.

"Are you sure?" I managed between ragged breaths, desperation clawing at my insides. I needed her affirmation, though every fiber of my being screamed that there was no turning back now.

Her eyes, dark pools in the dim light, held mine as she nodded once, decisively. It was all the permission my soul craved, and yet it was a consent that bore the weight of the world we were risking.

With a rough grip, I swept her up into my arms, her slight figure so much lighter than the burden of our actions. I carried her past the threshold of my bedroom, deliberately choosing the sanctity of my space over hers. Every step was laden with possession; with each footfall, I claimed her as mine in a way that transcended the physical.

The door clicked shut behind us, sealing away the rest of the world. Here in the shadows, where the silk sheets whispered promises and the darkness cloaked our sins, I laid her down with a tenderness that juxtaposed the storm raging within me.

As I worshipped the curves of her body with my lips, marking her with my kisses, her sighs filled the room. They were sounds of surrender, the sweetest symphony to my ears. She arched beneath me, giving herself over to the tempest of emotion, and I drowned in her like a man starved of air. Each touch was reverent, each movement an ode to the wildness that consumed us.

I thrust into her wet tight pussy, fucking hell it seemed like a glove filled with lotion, her intimate muscles clenched hard on my girth and I in turn teased her pulsing clit, while watching as her intimate juices squirted out over my thickness. She winced and whimpered at first, which is understandable.

I groaned.

"Darling you are mine you are the only one," I murmured which each steady thrust while alternating between sucking her right and her left large as diamonds and gorgeous nipple

She was not just under me, but with me, her body moving in perfect, passionate synchrony. In that moment, her youth and my experience clashed and melded until there was no divide, only the unity of two souls bound by a force stronger than the dangerous game we played. And as I marked her flesh as my own, I knew that whatever hellfire we'd have to walk through, Ivy was the one flame I couldn't extinguish.

* * *

I lay still, the aftershocks of our passion rippling through me as Ivy nestled closer. Her breath was even, her hand resting with a gentle possessiveness over my heart. She curled into me, her body a perfect fit against mine, and I felt her confidence, that peaceful certainty which she exuded like a warm blanket on a cold night. A silent promise seemed to float in the air between us, binding yet freeing.

My gaze fixed on the ornate plasterwork of the ceiling, intricate swirls and patterns that offered no answers to the turmoil inside me. We had crossed an invisible line drawn in the shadows of loyalty and betrayal, a line that, once breached, could never be retraced. The weight of what we had done settled heavily on my chest, more oppressive than any physical burden. It was a silent acknowledgement that our actions this night would shape our destinies in ways we couldn't yet fathom.

She traced patterns on my skin with her fingers, but the touch that had set my entire being on fire moments ago now burned with a different intensity, an intensity laced with foreboding. I knew there would be consequences; there always were in my world. Yet for the first time, I questioned if some prices were too high, even for the power and control I wielded.

A door clicking close by echoed faintly in the distance, a subtle reminder that the sanctuary of this room was an illusion. My mind flickered to the security cameras that surveilled every corner of my estate, a precaution turned betrayer at this moment. I slid out of bed from Ivy, careful not to disturb her sleep, and quietly got dressed..

I took a deep breath and exhaled.

Then I navigated the dim hallways with practiced ease, finding my way to the security room where banks of screens cast a ghostly glow.

There it was, a grainy image of Ivy and me leaving the bedroom, our connection unmistakable. No one was in the room to witness it now, but it was only a matter of time before eyes would pry and tongues would wag.

A few taps on the keyboard, a couple of clicks, and the footage dissolved into digital oblivion. As the screen blinked back to the live feed of an empty corridor, a definitive line was drawn in my mind. I had chosen my side. With that simple act of erasure, I had declared myself, fully and irrevocably, committed to whatever future lay with Ivy.

Gone was the calculated caution of a mafia don who played every angle. In its place was a man who had given in to the reckless gravity of desire and emotion. I was all in now, fucking come heaven or hellfire.

Chapter 5

Dominic

I woke with the empty sensation beside me, a cold expanse where warmth should have been. The sheets were a silent testament to the night before, twisted and disheveled, a stark contrast to the order that usually ruled my life. Ivy had left my bed before the first light crept through the curtains. I rose, muscles aching in a way that had nothing to do with my usual morning workout.

A soft mist draped the garden, awaiting the new day. There she was, amidst the roses and ivy, like some ethereal creature that didn't belong in my harsh reality.

Barefoot, her skin kissed by the emerging dawn, she hummed an unfamiliar tune. Her peace contrasted with my anxiety. She looked untouched by the passion that had consumed us mere hours ago. I wasn't; the memory of it clawed at my insides, leaving me raw.

Breakfast was a quiet affair, the clinking of silverware against china creating a fragile symphony.

The scent of fresh coffee did little to clear the fog in my head. Ivy sat across from me, her legs crossed beneath the table, her face alight with a mischief that spelled trouble. She reached for the salt, her fingers casually brushing mine. A spark shot up my arm.

"Careful," I growled, the warning rough in my throat. But she just smiled, that damn smile that could mean everything and nothing, and I felt the power of my world slipping through my fingers like sand. I knew then, with a certainty that sank like a stone in my gut, I had already lost. Whatever game we were playing, whatever rules I thought governed my life, she had changed them without even trying.

***

The sun had climbed a few more inches into the sky when I finally found my voice gravelly from the night's transgressions. "We keep this to ourselves," I said, the command brooking no argument. The garden around us felt like an accomplice, its blooms too bright, too silent.

"Until I'm safe," Ivy agreed, her gaze fixed on the labyrinth of green before her, a little smile playing on her lips as if she were privy to some secret joke. She didn't understand the gravity, or maybe she did and just didn't care.

"Temporary," I insisted, needing her to acknowledge the impermanence, the mistake of it all.

"Of course," she whispered, but her silence was louder than any promise she could make.

There was an unsettling certainty in her eyes that spoke of deeper roots, of something taking hold that wouldn't easily be uprooted.

Later, amidst the fortified walls of my office, the weight of responsibility settled heavily on my shoulders. My men, loyal soldiers in a war they didn't fully comprehend, stood before me. "Ivy's ex is sniffing around again," I lied through clenched teeth, hating myself for involving them in this deception. "I want eyes everywhere. No one gets within a block of this place without us knowing."

They nodded, the machinery of protection whirring to life with a sense of urgency. They didn't question the sudden escalation; trust in my judgment was implicit. But as they dispersed, carrying out orders with efficient haste, a cold sweat broke across my brow.

I was terrified, not of Ivy's past returning to claim her, but of someone discovering what she had become to me. It was a truth that would shatter my carefully constructed world, a vulnerability I couldn't afford. A weakness potent enough to bring the empire I had built to its knees.

***

I stalked through my estate, the air thick with secrets. The morning's light barely crept through the draped windows, casting elongated shadows that slithered along the walls like silent accusations. I had barely settled behind my desk when Dante, one of my most trusted enforcers, motioned from the doorway.

"Boss," he said, his voice a low rumble that seemed to echo off the marble floors, "we need to talk."

I met him in the dimly lit alcove, away from prying eyes and eager ears. His brow was creased with concern, a stark contrast to the perpetual calm he exuded.

"Dominic," Dante began, his gaze steady, "this thing with Ivy...it's got you twisted up. She's a distraction."

The air turned colder, denser. My hand twitched towards the gun holstered under my jacket. Threats to my empire were dealt with swiftly, without sentiment. But this was different; this was Ivy.

"Watch your words, Dante," I warned, my voice a lethal whisper. "She is not to be discussed or debated. This conversation never happened."

Dante held my gaze for a moment longer before nodding once, tight-lipped. He knew the line had been drawn; the message was clear—Ivy was untouchable.

As night descended and the house fell into a somber quietude, I tried to lose myself in the work that demanded my attention. But the numbers and reports blurred into insignificance against the backdrop of my thoughts. Her laughter echoed in the chambers of my mind, her touch branded onto my skin.

And then she was there, materializing like a vision at the threshold of my office. Ivy, wearing nothing but one of my shirts, the fabric hanging off her delicate frame, barely reaching mid-thigh. I watched, rapt, as she closed the distance between us with a grace that belied the storm she brought into my life.

"Dominic," she breathed, her voice a siren's call that left no room for resistance.

She climbed into my lap, her legs folding on either side of me with an intimacy that shattered any remaining resolve. The scent of her hair, a mix of jasmine and something uniquely Ivy, filled my senses. Her warmth seeped through the thin cotton, branding itself onto my very soul.

"Is this alright?" she asked, her breath ghosting across my cheek, her eyes searching mine for signs of the turmoil that churned within.

"More than alright," I murmured, my hands finding their way to her waist, anchoring her to me.

In that moment, the world outside my office ceased to exist. The dangers lurking in the shadows, the responsibilities weighing heavily upon my shoulders, they all faded into obscurity. There was only Ivy, a tempest disguised as tranquility, nestled in my arms as if she belonged nowhere else. And for the first time, I allowed myself to believe that perhaps she did.

* * *

Her fingers traced the scars on my back, a path of whispered secrets against my skin. "You're a dangerous game, Ivy," I blurted.

She tilted her head, locks of hair cascading down her shoulder like a curtain of night. A mischievous glint sparkled in her eyes, daring me to plunge further into the abyss. "Then lose," she said, her voice low and confident.

I kissed her, sealing our silent promise. The kiss was a flame igniting a fire that had been smoldering beneath the surface, threatening to consume us. It spoke of surrender, of battles lost willingly. My heart thundered against my chest, a drumbeat to the rhythm of our entwined souls.

We moved together, a dance of shadows and desire upon the cold, hard surface of my desk. Our movements were reckless, yet we remained quiet, stifling the sounds of our union as if the darkness itself demanded our silence. She was a melody of soft sighs and tender touches, a contrast to the harsh reality waiting just beyond the walls of my sanctuary.

As the first light of dawn crept through the blinds, casting bars of gold across the room, a realization settled over me with the weight of all my transgressions. Ivy, with her impish smile and unyielding spirit, was not a mistake to be buried and forgotten. She was a vulnerability, a chink in my armor I would defend with my last breath. In her embrace, I found a weakness I'd kill to protect.

Chapter 6

Ivy

I lingered in the dimly lit hallway, my back pressed against the cool wall as I listened for the telltale footsteps. Dominic's shadow stretched across the floor before he appeared, moving with a silence that belied his size. He possessively took my hand. We didn't speak; words were dangerous luxuries we couldn't afford.

The air between us was charged, every stolen touch like a live wire sparking against my skin. In the kitchen, our hands brushed as he passed me a glass of water, a gesture mundane to any observer but loaded with meaning for us. The cold liquid did nothing to quell the heat that his proximity evoked.

Later, in the car, his hand rested on my thigh under the cover of darkness as the city lights whizzed by. I could feel the weight of his gaze even though I kept my eyes fixed on the passing scenery. The secrecy of it all, the thrill of hiding plain sight, ignited something reckless within me.

From a distance, I caught him watching me once when I wasn't meant to notice. There was an intensity in his eyes that made my heart skip.

It was as if he could see how seamlessly I had slipped into his world of shadows and silence. The realization should have been terrifying, instead, it lured me deeper into the web we were weaving.

He stood at the edge of the room during one of those endless gatherings, a glass of whiskey in his hand, never touching his lips.

His focus was on me, even as others vied for his attention. His expression was unreadable, but I knew him well enough now to catch the flicker of fear that he quickly masked. A fear not for himself, but for what I was becoming within his dark orbit.

At night, I would lie awake and replay these moments, trying to piece together the man who held power over so many yet seemed powerless to the chaos I brought into his life.

Each memory was a brushstroke in the portrait of a man who was both my captor and my sanctuary. And as much as I wanted to deny it, I knew I was changing, shifting shape to fit into the spaces between his world and mine.

* * *

The silk of his shirt whispered against my skin as I padded barefoot down the opulent hallway, my heart hammering a wild rhythm. It was our game, this dance of near discovery, the thrill of stolen glances and touches that left me breathless. But today was different.

The air felt heavier, charged with an electricity that spoke of danger lurking just beneath the surface.

"Isabella?" His voice, usually so commanding, held a note of warning as he caught sight of me wearing nothing but his oversized shirt. I paused, turning to him with a practiced smile that didn't quite reach my eyes.

"Relax, Dominic," I murmured, even as the lie tasted like ash on my tongue. "It's just us here."

But it wasn't just us; the house was never truly ours. There were always ears listening, eyes watching—especially Dante's. With every question he asked, the noose tightened, and I knew it was only a matter of time before he pieced together the truth.

As I continued toward the kitchen, the ringtone of my phone sliced through the silence, a shrill reminder of the life I was supposed to lead. My father's name flashed across the screen, and my breath hitched. One slip, one hint of where I truly was, and everything would come crashing down.

"Hello, Daddy," I answered, keeping my voice light, schooling my features into a mask of innocence. Dominic's presence loomed large behind me, a silent sentinel.

"Where are you, Ivy? You sound...different." The suspicion in my father's tone was like a physical blow, but I was learning fast, adapting to the necessity of deceit.

"Just out for a walk, clearing my head." The ease with which the falsehood slipped from my lips sent a shiver down my spine. In the corner of my eye, I saw Dominic's jaw clench, his discomfort mirroring my own.

"Be careful, sweetheart," my father said, his words a command disguised as concern. "And come home soon."

"Of course, Daddy. I love you." Another lie, another link in the chain that bound me to this life.

I ended the call and glanced up at Dominic, his dark eyes a storm of emotions I couldn't decipher. Fear, perhaps, or was it something deeper?

"Dominic," I whispered, reaching for him, needing to bridge the gap that had opened between us.

He took a step back, a small denial that spoke volumes. "You're getting too good at lying," he said, his voice rough. "It scares me, Ivy."

"Then let me go," I challenged, even though we both knew it was an impossibility.

"Never," he replied, the word a promise and a threat all at once.

Before I could respond, Dante's shadow fell across the room, his gaze sharp and probing. "Dominic, can I have a word?"

I retreated to a safe distance, watching as the two men stepped into the study. The door couldn't muffle their voices, not completely. Words like "suspicious" and "danger" reached my ears, and I knew they were talking about me.

"Stay out of it, Dante," Dominic's voice carried authority, edged with a darkness that made even my blood run cold. "I'm warning you—back off."

"Or what?" Dante's challenge was met with silence, a tension that stretched taut between them.

"Or you'll find out exactly what I'm capable of," Dominic finally said, a low growl that promised retribution.

Their conversation ended with the sound of footsteps, and then Dante emerged, his eyes flicking to mine with a questioning look I couldn't quite interpret. He didn't speak, but his silence was louder than any accusation.

"Stay close, Ivy," Dominic ordered as he followed Dante out. "Very close."

The words wrapped around me like chains, a reminder of the gilded cage I now inhabited. I nodded, my resolve hardening. For in this world of shadows and lies, closeness wasn't just a command—it was survival.

* * *

The cold metal of the gun weighed heavy in my hand, a foreign object that Dominic insisted I learn to handle. "Steady," he murmured, his breath hot against my ear as his hands found my hips, guiding me with a gentle pressure that belied the strength in his touch. The sexual tension crackled between us like static, every correction, every shift bringing us closer.

"Focus on the target," he instructed, and I nodded, squaring my shoulders as I aimed down the sight. My finger curled around the trigger, hesitant at first, then firmer as determination settled in my bones. The gunshot echoed, a shockwave through the silence, and when the dust settled, my eyes widened at the sight of the bullet hole right through the center of the target.

"Perfect shot," he said, pride lacing his voice. Before I could react, his lips were on mine, a kiss tasting of power and promise that stole my breath away. When he pulled back, his stormy eyes searched mine, and I was lost in the tempest of him.

"Dominic," I started, my voice unsteady as the afterglow of our kiss lingered on my lips. "Tell me about your past, about the things you've done." It was a risk, prying into the shadows of his life, but I needed to understand the man who had become both my captor and my savior.

His gaze flickered, a shutter coming down as he considered what to reveal. "I've made choices, some harder than others," he began, his voice a low rumble that resonated within the empty shooting range. "I've protected my family, my people, at any cost."

"Any cost?" I pressed, my curiosity battling the fear of knowing too much.

"Power demands sacrifice, Ivy." He paused, his jaw clenching as if each word was a battle. "There are lines I've crossed that can't be uncrossed, debts paid in blood and loyalty."

I wanted more—more details, more truths—but the look in his eyes stopped me. This was Dominic laid bare as much as he'd allow, a man shrouded in darkness with glimpses of light that I found myself desperate to chase.

"Thank you for not lying," I said softly, touching his arm, feeling the muscle tense under my fingers.

"Never to you," he replied, the intensity of his vow wrapping around me like an embrace. But even as he spoke, I knew there were depths to

Dominic that I hadn't yet plumbed, secrets that lay buried beneath layers of necessity and survival.

In that moment, I realized the gravity of our connection, forged by force but bound by something more. And I wondered, in the heart of this gilded cage, if I would ever truly be ready for the weight of his world.

* * *

The cold steel of the gun still lingered on my fingertips as I lay in the dark, the sheets a barrier between Dominic's warmth and my shivering form.

Our breathing was a synchronized rhythm, filling the silence that cloaked the room like a heavy velvet curtain. The space between us felt like an ocean, vast and deep, yet I craved the shore of his touch.

"I'm not afraid of you," I whispered into the darkness, the words slipping out like a secret confession meant only for the night. There was no movement from him, no sign he'd even heard, but I knew he was awake, every line of his body rigid with unspoken thoughts.

His silence nestled into my chest, a haunting void where reassurance should have been. I wondered if he feared for me or because of me—the girl who wasn't supposed to be here, who wasn't supposed to know the passionless kiss of a trigger or the taste of a lie.

A soft buzz shattered the stillness, a harbinger of the storm that brewed beyond these walls. Dominic's hand moved, swift and silent, retrieving the phone that cast an ominous glow over the room. He read the message, his eyes narrowing, the muscle in his jaw ticking with tension.

"Your ex," he said, voice a low growl that sent shivers down my spine. "He's asking questions. Digging in places he shouldn't."

Panic fluttered in my chest, a caged bird desperate for escape. But it wasn't fear of my ex that fueled the frantic beating of my heart, it was the realization that his curiosity could unravel the fragile life I'd woven here with Dominic.

"Stay close to me," Dominic ordered, his tone leaving no room for argument. "Very close."

I nodded, understanding the gravity behind his command. This wasn't just about proximity; this was about survival. In this world, secrets were currency, and mine had just become a liability we couldn't afford.

Dominic shifted, closing the gap between us until his arm brushed against mine, a current of electricity connecting us in the quiet before dawn.

And in the shadows that danced across the walls, I saw the outline of our entwined fate: a tale of love and danger, written in whispers and warns.

Chapter 7

Ivy

I leaned against the kitchen island, the veins in the stone mirroring the tension in my body. Dominic paced before me like a caged beast, his dark eyes smoldering with an intensity that both scared and attracted me.

"Dominic, I can't keep living like this," I said, my voice steadier than I felt even though honestly I asked for this in the first place. "I need to breathe, to feel the sun on my face without a guard shadowing my every step."

He stopped pacing and fixed me with a glare that could freeze hell over. "This isn't about what you want, Ivy. It's about keeping you alive. My world isn't kind to vulnerabilities, and like it or not, you are mine."

His words stung, the implication clear: I was a liability, a weakness to be exploited. "I am not your property to be locked away," I shot back, anger flaring within me. "I can take care of myself."

"Can you?" He closed the distance between us in two strides, his presence engulfing me. His hand found the nape of my neck, grip firm, possessive. "You have no idea what they're capable of."

I moaned as he crushed his lips on mine, not soft or questioning but hard and punishing. This kiss wasn't about passion; it was a reminder of the danger, of his control, of the fact that he believed my freedom was a risk we couldn't afford.

I pushed him away, gasping for air, my heart pounding with a mix of desire and defiance. Before I could catch my breath, his phone buzzed ominously on the counter. The change in him was immediate. His body tensed, and a deep growl rumbled from his chest as he read the message.

"Damn it," he cursed under his breath, turning the screen toward me. A photo of me, taken from a distance as I stood by the window of the cafe just yesterday. How did I miss being watched?

"Who sent this?" I asked, fear creeping into my voice despite my resolve to appear unfazed.

"An enemy who knows how to hit where it hurts, the same one who you ran to me about," he replied, his jaw clenching. He grabbed his phone and began issuing commands like a general preparing for war. "I'm tightening security. No one gets near you without going through me first."

I watched as Dominic transformed from the man I was growing to care for into the ruthless leader of his dark empire. He moved through the house, barking orders into the phone, calling in favors from contacts I didn't dare ask about.

The opulent setting of our gilded cage seemed to mock me now, each luxury a reminder of the price paid in shadows and blood. The chandeliers overhead cast fractured light across Dominic's face, a mosaic of the turmoil undoubtedly raging within him.

As the weight of our situation settled over me like the heavy silk of the drapes, I realized my longing for freedom had just tightened the surrounding noose. Dominic's world wouldn't bend to my wishes; it would break us if we weren't careful. And yet, standing there, watching the man I couldn't help but feel drawn to protect me with such ferocity, a dangerous thought whispered through my mind: maybe some cages were worth the sacrifice.

* * *

I leaned against the cool marble of the kitchen island, my fingers tracing the intricate veining as if it could somehow distract me from the cage Dominic had just reinforced around my life. "I'm not some damsel," I said, my voice steady despite the tremor in my heart. "I can take care of myself."

Dominic was tense, his gaze fixed on the threatening photo spread across the granite countertop. The muscles of his jaw flexed, a visible sign of the storm brewing within him. "It's not about your strength," he said without turning. "It's about the savages outside these walls."

"Strength?" I scoffed, pushing away from the counter. "You think I don't know danger? My ex" I paused, swallowing the lump that formed in my throat, "he made sure I understood what cruelty looked like."

At the mention of my ex, Dominic spun around, his dark eyes flaring with a rage that felt palpable. He took a step toward me, each footfall heavy with lethal promise. "He breathes near you again, he dies," Dominic growled, the words slicing through the room with the sharpness of shattered glass.

Before I could respond, our argument reignited a firestorm of passion and panic. Dominic's shouts filled the space between us, echoing off the high ceilings as I stood defiantly before him. This wasn't just about protection; it was about control, and I fought back with every word, unwilling to surrender my last shred of autonomy.

In an instant, the distance vanished, and I was pinned against the wall, his hands framing my face with an intensity that stole my breath. His lips crashed against mine, a kiss that wasn't gentle or tentative. It was desperate, hungry, like he was drowning and I was the only lifeline he had left.

The kiss broke the surface of our fears, and for a moment, we clung to each other, the rest of the world falling away. Only his touch, fierce and unyielding, anchored me to the present, to the man whose darkness matched my own.

* * *

Dominic's touch scorched my skin, each caress more demanding than the last. Our ragged breaths tangled in the dimly lit room as we sought to erase the fear with a fervor that bordered on ferocity. His hands, those of a man who commanded empires, now roamed my body with a possessiveness that both thrilled and terrified me.

The silk sheets beneath us twisted with our movements, a testament to the intensity that drove us.

Sounds of passionate sex and the slapping sounds of our bodies moving together filled the air!

Freaking heck—

I was in for it now and there was no going back! I am in too deep in love with him.

"Fuck me," I pleaded. It wasn't a word I would normally use but perhaps this was the real me wanting to come out, no longer bound by mindless traditions or the fear from the past. He loved me like no one else did, he was sensual and experienced with his savage thrusts in and out my wanting wet tight slit.

We made love like two souls battling the darkness together, rough and unrelenting, desperate to find solace in the storm.

"Fuck I am coming Ivy! I want you to fucking have my baby, you are mine!" He growled. I nodded. Little gasps of pleasure escaped my lips as I came over and over again! My intimate muscles gripping his girth each time an over whelming intense orgasm seemed to wreck my entire being!

Dominic couldn't hold back any longer either. He tried holding back, gritting his teeth to stop but he couldn't. He came with a shout releasing his warmth like a storm into my wanting pleasure spot!

Panting from our release he kissed my lips and said, "you are mine forever, thank you Ivy."

I moaned as he kissed me one final time.

* * *

Afterward, I lay spent and panting, watching Dominic through half-lidded eyes. He prowled around the room, every muscle tensed like a coil ready to snap. His jaw clenched as he picked up his phone, thumbing through it with purpose. The surrounding air crackled with silent command. He spoke into the receiver, his voice low but filled with an authority that needed no amplification.

"Marco, it's time to dig deeper. Find out everything about her ex - where he's been, who he's talking to, what his next move is," Dominic instructed, his gaze never leaving mine. There was a promise in those eyes, a dark oath to protect what was his. But there were secrets there too, hidden just beneath the surface. Secrets he wasn't sharing with me yet.

He ended the call and came back to bed, his presence a heavy weight in the opulent room. I watched him, this enigmatic man who held my safety in one hand and my heart in the other. The unease stirred within me, sensing the truths he kept locked away. But for now, I pushed away the questions, letting the remnants of passion lull me into a restless sleep while Dominic stood watch, a silent sentinel against the threats lurking in the shadows.

* * *

I crept down the staircase. The house, with its lavish trappings, felt suffocating now, like a golden cage that glittered in the dim light. I paused midway, the murmur of voices snagging my attention. Dominic's deep timbre floated up from his study, the door ajar just a sliver. Curiosity pricked at me, and I edged closer.

"Keep it quiet, Marco. She can't know, not yet," he said, his voice a blade wrapped in velvet. There was a tension in his words, an unspoken urgency that sent chills down my spine.

I clutched the banister, my heart pounding against my ribs. Secrets. He had them, and they were about me. But I didn't confront him. Something shattered quietly inside me as I realized trust was a two-way street, and Dominic's lane was closed for maintenance.

With newfound resolve, I slipped outside into the night, my breath catching in the cool air. The guards were shadows themselves, their attention elsewhere. A thrill raced through me as I made it past them, a silent dance between freedom and folly.

I walked the streets alone, each step a declaration. My pulse sang with the danger of it, a sweet melody only those who have known captivity can truly appreciate. For the first time in weeks, I inhaled deeply without the scent of Dominic's cologne mingling with the air.

It wasn't long before the inevitable happened. My phone buzzed, and I knew without looking it was Dominic. His anger would be a tempest, his worry a storm surge. But as I rejected the call, I understood something profound. In his own twisted way, he needed me safe, needed me more than his empire, his control, his vendettas.

And just maybe, under the layers of darkness and power, there was a man who could learn to love without chains. But as I turned back toward the looming silhouette of our home, I wondered if we'd ever find the key to unlock that part of him together.

Chapter 8

Ivy

I thought I could push it.

Just a little. Just enough.

The mansion walls were closing in, and I couldn't breathe. I told myself I needed air, that I was just stepping out for a moment, not running. But maybe I was lying—to myself and to him.

The moment I reached for the front door, I felt it.

His presence.

Then his hand, firm around my wrist.

"Ivy." His voice was low, rough. "Where do you think you're going?"

"I needed air," I lied, not meeting his eyes.

"You asked me for protection," he said, his grip loosening but not releasing. "You don't get to change the rules just because you're restless."

"I didn't agree to be your prisoner."

"And I didn't take a vow I didn't mean." His jaw tightened, his eyes burning into me. "I don't half-ass promises. Not to your father. Not to you."

I opened my mouth to argue, to plead, to *something*, but he didn't give me the chance.

He turned, walked back to the room I'd been staying in, and opened the door.

"Get In."

I moved before my pride could argue.

"This is for your protection Ivy."

And with that he crushed his lips on mine. Then he teased my naughty wet spot to submission, freaking heck I responded wanting more. He didn't stop until I climaxed. Holy freaking heck why does he have this power over me?

And with that, he rose up, kissed my lips and walked out the door without a freaking word.

I gasped, the glanced at the oak door watching as the locks clicked.

The sound slammed into me, final and cruel, sealing my fate. He stood outside the door, his heavy breathing the only sign he hadn't left. I pounded my fists against the solid oak, each thud echoing through the lavish room that now trapped me.

"Dominic, open this door!" I screamed, my voice hoarse with desperation and fury. "You can't do this to me!"

On the other side, I could almost see his dark eyes clouded with a storm of emotions, his jaw set in that stubborn way that brooked no argument. He was terrified, of what I could do, of what could happen to us both. But his fear manifested in anger, in control. And he was unyielding.

"Dammit, Dominic! You said you cared about me!" The words were sharp, aimed to wound as much as his betrayal had cut deep into my heart.

There was no reply, just the receding footsteps that told me he was walking away, leaving me caged like some prized possession too dangerous to be left unattended. I slid down beside the door, my energy draining as the realization sunk in. He wouldn't relent. Not now.

For two days, I was a ghost in my life. I paced the confines of my luxurious prison, tracing patterns on the silk wallpaper, the fabric of my world reduced to these four walls. I cried until there were no tears left, until my soul felt as parched as my eyes.

Through it all, I knew he watched. The cameras, discreetly tucked into the corners of the ceiling, were his eyes. I could feel the weight of his gaze, cold and relentless. On the security feed,

I was just another item under surveillance, another asset to protect. It was dehumanizing.

I tried to reach him through that electronic barrier. I'd stare directly at the lens, willing him to understand, to see the pain he was inflicting. But the screens don't transmit feelings; they just display images, devoid of context, of emotion.

Then, abruptly, I stopped. No more pleading looks, no more silent cries for understanding. I sat on the edge of the bed, my posture poised but my spirit defeated. I went still, conserving what little dignity I had left. In that stillness, I found a frightening sense of clarity. This was how he saw me, something to be locked away, controlled, kept at a distance.

And as I remained motionless, a statue in a gilded cage, I felt the last threads of hope fray and snap. What was love if it came with shackles? What was desire if it imprisoned rather than freed?

I let the silence envelop me, a cocoon that was part refuge, part tomb. Inside, I wrestled with the sorrow of lost illusions and the bitter taste of a love that smothered rather than soared.

* * *

The door to my gilded prison creaked open, and his heavy footsteps echoed across the hardwood floor. Dante stood at the threshold, his face a map of concern etched into his weathered features. "Dominic, we need to talk."

I watched from behind the locked door, a silent observer to their confrontation. My heart thrummed in my ears as I leaned closer, desperate for a sign of what was to come.

"Her spirit's breaking," Dante said, his voice low but unwavering. "You can't keep her like this. It's not right."

"Enough!" Dominic exploded, the word a thunderclap that shook the foundation of our fragile existence. "This is my house, my rules. You don't like it? There's the door."

Dante clenched his jaw, the lines around his eyes deepening with the weight of unspoken thoughts. He turned to leave, casting a last, lingering look in my direction. His eyes held an apology that couldn't be voiced, a silent solidarity with my plight.

The silence hung heavy after he left, filled with unsaid words and unresolved tensions. It wasn't until the next day that I found the courage to speak, my voice emerging calm and clear despite the chaos churning within me.

"Dominic," I began, my gaze steady on the camera that had become my constant watcher, "if you treat me like a prisoner, then you don't deserve me."

The words fell into the room like stones into still water, rippling through the air and leaving an indelible mark on the moment. I could almost feel him on the other side of the lens, his presence a dark cloud that blotted out the sun.

There was no response, no sign that my declaration had reached him. But I knew it had pierced his armor, even if only by the smallest of margins. Because in that instance, I wasn't just the young woman who'd fallen into his world; I was the force that dared to defy it.

***

I slid the window open, the cool night air kissing my skin like a promise of freedom. My heart thrummed against my ribs as I climbed out, every movement deliberate, quiet. The sprawling estate that had been a gilded cage loomed behind me, its opulent silhouette mocking my desperation. I kept to the shadows, my feet whispering across the dew-kissed grass as I made for the gate—the boundary between this life and the unknown.

The iron bars felt cold and unyielding beneath my fingers, a stark contrast to the warmth of the tears that traced silent paths down my cheeks. "You said one night," my voice broke the silence, a ghostly murmur to the night. "I gave you everything."

"Please, Ivy." His voice shattered the stillness from behind me, a plea wrapped in a velvet growl. There was no anger this time, only raw need. I turned to find Dominic standing there, his dark eyes wide with something akin to fear. "Don't go."

I shook my head, the scald of betrayal burning my throat. "I can't stay here, locked away because you are concerned about what might happen. That's not living, Dominic."

He stepped closer, the distance between us charged with a thousand unspoken words. His hand reached out but stopped short of touching me. "I know—I messed up. But you're not just anyone." His voice cracked, a rare glimpse of the man behind the mafia don's façade. "You're the only one."

His admission hung in the air, a fragile truth that tethered me to the spot. I saw him then—not the hardened criminal, not the untouchable leader, but Dominic, the man with a heart fighting its way through layers of darkness. The man who, for the first time, looked at me and saw more than an obligation, more than a secret to be kept. He saw me as I wanted to be seen: someone worth breaking the rules for, someone worth the risk.

"Dominic," I whispered, the fight seeping from my bones. His name was a white flag, a surrender to the complexities of our twisted reality. And as he closed the gap, taking my hands in his, I knew that escape wasn't found beyond the gate, it was standing right in front of me, begging me to stay.

***

The key turned in the lock with a soft click that echoed like a verdict in the silence of my room. I held my breath, half expecting another round of futile pleas and accusations. Instead, Dominic pushed the door open, his frame filling the space with a presence that made my heart lurch. There was no anger in his eyes, no stern lines carving his features into the formidable don I'd come to both fear and crave.

"Your door will remain unlocked," he said, voice barely above a whisper. "You're free to go wherever you wish within the estate."

His words, simple and devoid of conditions, wrapped around me like a promise. I searched his face for any sign of the man who had locked me away, but all I saw was raw vulnerability—a sight so rare, it felt as though I was witnessing the shedding of an impenetrable armor. He was granting me more than just freedom; he was offering me his trust, laying it at my feet like a penitent.

"Dominic," I murmured, my voice foreign in its gentleness. I took a tentative step forward, watching as he visibly tensed, prepared for rejection.

"Stay," he said, swallowing hard. "Please."

It wasn't a command. It was a plea from the depths of a heart too long shrouded in shadows. My resolve crumbled, not because I had nowhere else to go, but because the man before me was baring his soul, and I couldn't look away.

"I'll stay," I whispered back, sealing our unspoken pact.

That night, as we came together once more, the world outside faded into insignificance. His touch was tender, reverential, as if each caress was an apology and a vow woven together. Our movements were slow, charged with an intensity that had nothing to do with passion and everything to do with connection. Each kiss, each sigh, each entwining of limbs spoke of things deeper than desire of wounds healing and walls crumbling.

I was no longer the girl caught in the crossfire of a life she never asked for. In his arms, I became the axis upon which his world spun, the silent witness to the transformation of a man feared by many but truly known by none. As he whispered my name like a prayer, I knew that this was where I belonged, not as a secret tucked away in the dark, but as the beating heart of his existence, the light guiding him through the labyrinth of his own making.

In the quiet aftermath, as dawn's first light crept across the opulent expanse of the room, I watched Dominic sleep. The lines of stress and power that marked his face seemed softer, almost peaceful. I traced the contours of his features with my eyes, memorizing the way the morning sun danced across his skin, casting him in hues of gold and warmth.

And in that moment, between one heartbeat and the next, I allowed myself to believe in the possibility of us, not just as rivals, but as two souls tethered by a choice to defy the odds.

Chapter 9

Ivy

I twisted the gold band on my finger, a nervous habit I'd picked up since the night Dominic had slipped it onto my skin. The ring was a shackle, a promise, a lifeline—all in one. We were two shadows flitting through a world that wasn't kind to creatures like us; we trusted no one, not even the silence between our breaths.

The kitchen of the safe house was opulent, a stark contrast to the thick tension that hung in the air like the scent of gunpowder. Marble countertops gleamed under the low light, and every surface seemed to whisper secrets of wealth and hidden knives. We moved around each other with a cautious choreography—Dominic at the stove, me by the counter chopping vegetables.

"Hand me the salt," he said without turning, voice calm as if we were an old married couple instead of fugitives bound by necessity. I obliged, brushing past him, my senses alert to the warmth emanating from his body.

"Dominic, how do you know when it's done?" I asked, nodding toward the simmering saucepan.

He glanced at me, a flicker of something in his eyes, before he schooled his expression back to indifference. "When the sauce sticks to the spoon, like this." He lifted the wooden ladle, demonstrating.

"Let me try." I reached for the spoon, but instead of handing it over, he used it to draw a line of red sauce down my arm.

"Hey!" I protested, but the shock quickly morphed into amusement. Without thinking, I dipped my fingers into the sauce and smeared a dollop onto his cheek.

Dominic stilled, his dark gaze locking onto mine. A beat passed—one, two—before the corners of his mouth twitched. Suddenly, he was laughing, the sound rich and unexpected. It was the first time I'd heard it, and it reverberated through the cold room like a promise of spring after a harsh winter.

"Brat," he said, but there was warmth there, a crack in the armor he wore like a second skin.

And then he kissed me—with the sauce still on his face. The taste was sweet, and spicy, just like the man who held me close. It was messy and perfect, and for a moment, I forgot about the danger, the blood, and the debts to be paid. In that stolen second, we were just Ivy and Dominic, laughing and kissing in a kitchen that could've been anywhere.

***

I wiped my hands on a dishcloth, the laughter from moments before still lingering in the air like an echo. Dominic leaned against the marble countertop, his eyes no longer dancing with humor but clouded over with something distant and heavy.

"Dominic?" I ventured, cautious to tread into the silence that had fallen between us.

He glanced up, the ghost of a smile fading as quickly as it came. "My mother," he began, his voice a low rumble, "she was the first person I couldn't save." His words hung in the kitchen, each syllable laced with regret.

I felt a twinge in my chest, seeing him like this—vulnerable. The ever-present aura of strength and control seemed to slip away, revealing the man beneath the mobster. "What happened to her?"

"Wrong place, wrong time," he said, his gaze slipping past me to some unforgotten memory. "She got caught in a crossfire meant for me."

I reached out, my fingertips brushing his arm. The muscles beneath his skin were steel, yet they trembled under my touch. "You were just a kid, Dominic. There was nothing you could have done."

He shook his head, the shadows of the past playing across his features. "Doesn't change the fact that she's gone because of me."

Before I could reply, the shrill ring of my phone shattered the solemnity of our exchange. My heart leaped into my throat. It was a sound we'd grown to dread—a herald of potential exposure. I snatched the device from the counter, and my blood ran cold at the caller ID flashing on the screen: Dad.

"Shit," I hissed, swiping to answer the call. My mind raced, trying to conjure up a believable setting, a façade of normalcy.

"Hey, Dad," I said, my voice artificially bright.

"Hi, sweetheart! How are you? I thought I'd see how you're doing," he chirped, oblivious to the danger his call posed.

"Great, everything's great," I lied, my eyes darting to Dominic.

He understood instantly, his instincts honed by years of living on a knife edge. In a swift, fluid motion, he crouched down behind the kitchen island, effectively vanishing from view.

"Are you sure? You look tense, honey. Where are you?" my father pressed, his face filled with concern on the tiny screen.

"Uh, just visiting a friend. We're about to have dinner," I stammered, angling the camera away from any incriminating background. "It's been a long day; you know how it is."

"Okay, just checking in. Love you, Ivy."

"Love you too, Dad." I ended the call and let out a breath I didn't realize I'd been holding.

"Close call," Dominic muttered, rising from his hiding spot, his expression unreadable.

"Too close," I agreed, my pulse still racing. "We need to be more careful."

"Agreed," he said, and there was a new understanding between us—an acknowledgment of the delicate wire we walked together.

***

The night hugged us in its inky cloak as we left the safety of our hideout, and the city's distant lights cast a soft glow over the water. Dominic's hand, warm and steady, clasped mine as he led me down a path that only he seemed to know, winding between the trees until we emerged onto a pebbled shore.

"Wow," I whispered, the sound swallowed by the vast expanse before us. The moon, a silver sliver in the sky, reflected on the gentle waves, turning them into ribbons of light. Dominic had brought me to a place that felt untouched, private—where the rest of the world couldn't reach us.

I turned to look at him, his profile etched against the night. "This is beautiful," I said, my voice barely above a breath. He just nodded, his eyes fixed on the horizon, a man always watching for threats even in moments of peace.

We sat on the cool stones, the water lapping at our feet, wrapping us in solitude. It was here, under the stars, away from the chaos that had become our life, that I found the courage to speak my truth.

"Dominic, I want this—a life with you, not just hiding, but living."

He remained silent, staring out at the water, his jaw tightening. The words hung between us, heavy with implications he wasn't ready to accept, let alone reciprocate. A part of me knew it was too much to ask for a future when we were still so entangled in our past.

Before the silence could consume us, footsteps crunched on the gravel behind us. Dante, Dominic's second-in-command, materialized from the shadows like a wraith, his eyes sharp and accusing.

"Ivy," he began, his tone dripping with reproach. "You're becoming a distraction. Dominic has responsibilities; he can't afford to lose focus because of you."

I stood facing him squarely. His presence, once intimidating, now spurred something fierce within me. "Listen to me, Dante," I said, my voice cold, a surprising calm settling over me. "I am not some liability or damsel in distress. If anything, I am the weapon you didn't realize you had. So don't think for a second that I'll let anyone—not even you—threaten what we have."

Dante's eyes narrowed, and I could see the gears turning in his head as he reassessed me. There was a lethal edge to my words, and clearly it struck a nerve.

"Understood," he replied after a tense pause, his tone slightly more respectful. He glanced at Dominic, who hadn't moved an inch through our exchange, then stepped back, disappearing into the darkness as quietly as he had arrived.

Dominic finally spoke, his voice low. "Ivy..."

I sat back down, my heart racing with adrenaline. Whether it was the threat of discovery or the confrontation with Dante, I realized that in this world, strength was the only currency—and I had just proven my worth.

***

The silence of the night wrapped around us as we slipped back into the sanctuary of our hideout. Dominic's hand, warm and steady, guided me through the half-lit corridors that had become our maze of safety. We moved like phantoms between the shadows, a dance we mastered.

We were almost to the room we now shared when he stopped abruptly, his back rigid. I could tell from the slight tilt of his head that he was listening for something—perhaps the silent whispers of danger that seemed to stalk us at every turn. He laughed, a deep, rich sound that shook his whole body. The unexpected noise broke through the silence, warming the cold walls around us.

"Dominic?" I asked, puzzled by this sudden outburst.

He turned to face me, the ghost of a smile still playing on his lips. "I just heard about your little standoff with Dante," he said, eyes glinting with amusement. "You're dangerous."

My heart skipped a beat, not expecting him to find out so quickly. A flush of warmth spread through my chest, partly from pride, partly from the sheer relief of seeing him laugh. "I learned from the best," I shot back, the corners of my mouth lifting despite the unease that often clung to my thoughts.

The softness I glimpsed in his gaze told me he appreciated the irony. There we stood, two souls cut from the same cloth of survival, each recognizing the other's hard-won scars.

As we entered the room, the weight of the day began settling on my shoulders. The opulent space, with its heavy drapes and plush carpets, felt more like a cage than a refuge, yet it was here with Dominic that I found moments of respite.

We didn't speak as we prepared for bed, the routine familiar and oddly comforting. The tension that always lingered beneath my skin eased as I watched him move through the room, a silent sentinel keeping watch over our fragile peace.

Finally, under the cover of darkness, we lay down together. His arm encircled me, pulling me close, and I nestled into the curve of his body. Every breath he took seemed to sync with mine, and in that simple act of sharing air, we wove a cocoon around ourselves.

For the first time since we'd been thrown together in this tumultuous existence, I felt the edge of something like tranquility. The outside world, with all its threats and chaos, faded to a dull murmur against the steady rhythm of Dominic's heartbeat.

And there, in the quiet before dawn, with our breaths mingling and our limbs entwined, it felt like we were more than the sum of our parts. More than the girl who had been forced to grow up too fast, and the man burdened by a legacy of blood and duty. In each other's arms, we were just Ivy and Dominic, two people daring to believe in the possibility of peace—even if it was only a whisper in the dark.

Chapter 10
Dominic

The door clicked shut, the echo trailing off into the silent expanse of the marble-floored foyer. Marco's heavy footsteps had a way of making even the grandeur of our hideout seem mundane. He approached with that look in his eyes—the one that spelled trouble before his lips parted.

"Boss," he said, his voice low and urgent. "We've got word that Ivy's ex is gearing up for something big. Details are still foggy, but it ain't gonna be pretty."

I nodded, absorbing the news with a practiced calm that belied the storm brewing inside me. "Keep an eye on it, Marco. I want to know the moment you have something solid."

"Of course." He paused, as if expecting more, but I dismissed him with a tilt of my head, my mind already racing through scenarios, strategies, contingencies.

Ivy was upstairs, blissfully unaware of the impending threat. I made the call then and there; she didn't need to know—not yet. The weight of her safety pressed down on me like a leaden cloak, and I shouldered it alone. It was better this way.

Later, in the dim warmth of the oak-paneled den, her father sat across from me, swirling a glass of whiskey that caught the light from the fire. His jovial nature seemed out of place in our world of shadows and secrets.

"Dominic, my boy," he began, a smirk playing on his lips, "you must tell me your secret. Ever since Ivy's been under your watchful eye, she's turned into a quiet little dove. I haven't seen her this tame since she was in pigtails."

The amber liquid in my glass quivered as I brought it to my lips. His words hit closer than he knew, and I fought to keep my composure as I took a slow sip, the whiskey burning its way down. A cough threatened to betray my sudden discomfort, but I swallowed it along with the smoky heat.

"Perhaps she's just maturing," I offered, my voice steady despite the tightness in my chest. The irony wasn't lost on me—his daughter, the wild-spirited Ivy, confined within the walls I'd built around her for her own protection. "She goes by Ivy now."

He laughed it off. "Good I will call her Ivy, but she is Isabelle."

"Yes Ivy for protection," I lied. "Like I said earlier she's grown up."

"Ah, yes, maybe so, my baby Isabelle." He chuckled, oblivious to the double entendre, and raised his glass in a mock salute. "To growing up," he toasted, and I echoed the sentiment with a strained smile.

"Indeed," I replied, "to growing up."

But in my heart, the toast felt more like a solemn vow—a promise to shield Ivy from the chaos her past threatened to unleash upon us both.

* * *

Creeping silently through the dimly-lit corridor, I strained my ears to catch the low, muffled voices coming from the study. The heavy oak door was ajar just enough to let their words slip through like tendrils of smoke, curling and twisting into my consciousness. My father's laughter was a familiar rumble, but it was the undercurrent of something unsaid that made my pulse quicken.

"Growing up," Dominic's voice resonated, smooth and controlled, though I could almost feel the tension lacing each word. "Indeed."

I lingered in the shadows, the plush carpet beneath my feet muffling my presence. As they continued to talk, the atmosphere became dense with unspoken truths, tangling around me, drawing tighter. Something about the way Dominic spoke, the careful modulation of his tone, told me he was holding back a storm behind a calm facade.

"Anyway, thank you for looking after her, Dominic," my father said, a note of sincerity threading through his voice. "You've been good for Ivy."

"Of course," Dominic replied, and I imagined the subtle nod that would accompany his words. "She means a lot to me."

A sudden chill tiptoed down my spine as I realized there was more weight to their conversation than mere pleasantries—my father's intuition was sharper than either of us gave him credit for.

Before I could process it further, Dominic emerged from the study, closing the door quietly behind him. His eyes found mine instantly, dark pools reflecting a silent warning. He approached, and the air between us crackled with an intensity that made my heart skip.

"Ivy," he began, his voice barely above a whisper, "you need to stay out of sight for a while."

The command stoked a fire in my belly, a mix of frustration and fear. But the gravity in his gaze quelled the urge to argue. There was no room for dissent in his stance, his aura exuding authority and concern in equal measure.

"Fine," I conceded, biting the inside of my cheek to keep my mounting emotions at bay. "But only because I trust you."

He nodded once, solemn, and placed a firm hand on my shoulder. "It's for the best. For your safety."

As he walked away, the certainty of his steps did little to ease the growing tension coiled within me. Left alone in the hallway, I felt the weight of his request—and my compliance—settle on my shoulders like a mantle, heavy with the promise of secrets yet to unfold.

* * *

The chill of the marble floors seeped through the soles of my feet, a stark reminder of the coldness growing in my chest. Dominic's back was a wall of silence as he poured over documents at his desk, his focus unyielding. I hovered in the doorway, the need to confront him gnawing at me like a starving rat.

"Dominic," I said, my voice steady despite the tremors inside me. "You can't keep doing this—shutting me out, cloaking everything in secrecy."

He didn't look up, and that indifference stoked my anger further. My fists clenched at my sides, nails digging into my palms.

"Talk to me," I demanded, striding into the room. "I deserve to know what's happening."

Finally, he lifted his head, his expression carved from stone. "It's not your concern, Ivy."

"Not my concern?" I spat the words, incredulous. "My ex is plotting something, my father is onto us, and you think it's not my concern?"

His chair scraped against the floor as he stood, towering over me. The air shifted, heavy with the storm brewing between us.

"You don't understand the risks," he said, his voice a low growl.

"Then make me understand, damn it!" Tears bristled at the corners of my eyes, but I refused to let them fall.

For a moment, we stood locked in a silent battle of wills, the tension humming like a live wire. Then, something in him broke. He closed the distance, wrapping his arms around me in an embrace that was both protective and possessive.

"Mi Amor," he murmured into my hair, his breath hot on my scalp. "I'm sorry."

My resolve crumbled as I melted into him, the fight draining away. We moved together, a tangle of limbs and raw emotion, finding our way to the bathroom where the promise of steam and oblivion beckoned.

Water cascaded over us, washing away the harsh words and leaving tenderness in their wake. He traced the bruises on my skin souvenirs from a life lived dangerously close to the edge. Each touch was an apology, each kiss a plea for forgiveness.

"I should have told you," he whispered against my lips, his voice thick with regret.

"Tell me now," I urged, my fingers weaving through his wet hair, pulling him closer.

In the shower's embrace, we found solace in one another, our bodies speaking the language of reconciliation. As the steam enveloped us, the world outside ceased to exist. There was only the heat, the water, and the unspoken promises that danced in the droplets streaming down our entwined figures.

He slid his hands on my waist, hot and hungry, even under the water. I leaned back against him, my skin slick, his chest firm against my back. I could feel him—hard, thick, pressed right against me—and it made my thighs clench.

"You're not even pretending to behave," I whispered, tilting my head so he could kiss my neck.

"I was never planning to," he growled, lips brushing my ear.

He slid his hand up to my breast, squeezing like he couldn't get enough of me. His other hand drifted lower, teasing between my legs, slow and maddening. I moaned, biting my lip, gripping the tiled wall in front of me.

"Dominic—"

"Say it," he said, voice low and filthy.

"I want you," I breathed.

And that was all he needed. He spun me around and pinned me to the wall, water cascading over his shoulders, dripping down his abs like something out of a fantasy. I wrapped my legs around him without thinking. He slid inside me in one hard, perfect thrust.

God.

The tile was cold against my back, but I barely noticed. All I could feel was him—his cock pounding into me, his mouth claiming mine, his fingers digging into my hips. The sound of skin slapping and the water pounding only made it filthier. Hotter.

"You feel so good," I gasped, nails dragging down his back.

"Look at me," he said, voice rough. "Look at how wrecked you are for me."

I did. And he was right. I was wrecked. Drenched. Desperate. So close.

He hit that spot again and again until I couldn't hold it back. I came hard, trembling around him, crying out his name. He followed right after, groaning into my neck, every muscle in his body tensed.

We stood there for a second, breathing heavy, tangled together under the spray. I knew in that instant our bond as crazy as it sounds would never be broken.

* * *

A day later

The ink bled into the paper, a stark contrast to the pristine white it marred. I sat at the ornate writing desk that now felt like an altar for my confessions—a place where the truth battled with loyalty and love. I trembled as I scribbled the words that could change everything.

"Dear Father," I began, the salutation a shaky foundation for the avalanche of secrets I held back. My heart was a traitor, pounding against my chest as if urging me to spill every sin. The tip of the pen hovered above the page, indecision a heavy cloak on my shoulders.

I knew what revealing everything to him would mean—the risk, the potential fallout. Yet, there was also the weight of the unspoken, the distance that had crept between us since I found myself caught in Dominic's darkened world. It was this same distance that gnawed at me now, begging to be bridged by honesty.

"Things have been complicated lately," I wrote, the understatement of the year. How could I tell him about the forced proximity, the way Dominic's presence both suffocated and soothed me? How could I explain the twisted paths we'd taken, the lines we'd crossed?

I paused, the letter half-written, my mind a tempest of doubt. Could I really lay bare the complexities of my life with Dominic, the man who commanded silence and demanded loyalty with an iron fist wrapped in velvet?

The door creaked open, and my breath hitched. Dominic stood there, his silhouette framed by the doorway, eyes scanning the room until they landed on the letter. His expression was unreadable, but the air shifted, charged with an energy that spelled destruction.

He strode across the room, purpose in every step. Before I could react, he plucked the letter from the desk, his fingers grazing mine, sending an unwelcome shiver up my spine. I watched, frozen, as he scanned the words, his brow furrowing ever so slightly.

"Dominic, please," I started, but the plea stayed still within me. He turned toward the fireplace, where flames danced with deceptive cheerfulness. With a flick of his wrist, he released the letter, allowing it to flutter like a wounded bird before it was consumed by the fire.

"Better this way," he said, his voice low and devoid of warmth. "Your father doesn't need to know."

But I needed him to know. And as I watched the edges of the paper curl and blacken, the truth within turning to ash, I realized Dominic once again decided for me. The letter was gone, unread, its existence erased by the very man who claimed to protect me.

A silent scream filled the space where the words had been, and I understood then that the ink wasn't the only thing bleeding; it was us, our already fragile bond slowly hemorrhaging under the weight of secrets and lies.

Chapter 11
Dominic

The silent alarm in my office was a whisper of danger, a digital ghost that flickered across my screen without sound. It spelled treachery as a name I hadn't expected to see again—her ex. My men knew nothing of silence or subtlety, but they obeyed when I commanded them to follow, not kill. Not yet. The traitor's blood would stay warm in his veins a while longer.

From the moment I'd read the name, a frost had settled over me, creeping into the spaces between my ribs and icing over the warmth Ivy usually kindled there. I could sense her watching me as I gazed out the window, pretending to admire the city lights that sprawled like a kingdom at my feet. But it wasn't admiration that held me; it was the tightening noose of strategy and suspicion.

"Dominic," she said, her voice like the brush of silk against skin. "What's happened? You are miles away."

I turned from the window, meeting her emerald eyes that always seemed to strip me bare. She stood framed by the opulence of our room, the gold and velvet accents that adorned our private world, yet none of it could distract from the worry etched into her delicate features.

"Nothing important," I lied, my voice betraying none of the turmoil that gnawed at my insides. But she knew me too well—too intimately.

"Dominic, don't do this," she pressed, stepping closer until I could almost feel the heat of her body. "You've been different since you locked yourself in here. Tell me what's wrong."

I studied her face, the way her brow furrowed with concern, the slight quiver of her lip that suggested fear. How could I explain her past had crawled into my world, threatening the fragile peace we'd built? How could I tell her that the man she once loved now walked among my enemies?

"Sometimes things happen in my business that are better left unsaid," I told her, reaching out to tuck a stray lock of hair behind her ear. Her skin was soft beneath my fingertips, reminding me of all that was gentle in a life so often defined by brutality.

"Dominic," she whispered, closing the distance until we were a breath apart. "You can trust me. Whatever it is, we'll face it together."

Her words were a balm, but also a blade—soothing even as they cut through my defenses. I wanted to confide in her, to lean on her strength and let her share the burden of leadership and legacy that weighed on my shoulders. But some truths were too heavy to share, even with the woman who owned my heart.

"Trust that I'm handling it," I said, my voice firm despite the ache that accompanied the lie. The tension between us was a tangible thing, a dark cloud in our gilded cage.

Ivy's gaze didn't waver, but I saw the resignation in her eyes, the acceptance of my half-truths as she stepped back, putting space between us once more.

"Okay, Dominic," she said softly, and though the words were acquiescence, the steel in her tone told me that this wasn't over. Not for her. And not for me.

* * *

Dominic

I stood in our lavish dining hall, the clink of fine crystal and inaudible murmurs of conversation drifting through the air like errant whispers. Tonight, we were hosting a dinner for allies, and

Ivy was at my side, her dress a deep emerald that made her eyes gleam with an inner fire.

"Dominic, you're brooding again," she chided softly, her fingers brushing mine before she turned to greet a pair of guests with the grace of royalty. She had insisted on knowing what darkened my thoughts, and I had no choice but to let her glimpse the storm clouds on my horizon.

"Your ex, he's back." The words felt like shards of glass in my mouth.

Her face paled for a moment, but then she composed herself with that resilient poise I admired so fiercely. "You won't... Please, tell me you won't act against him."

I looked into those beseeching eyes and caged the beast within that howled for vengeance. "I promise," I lied, feeling the weight of my deceit settle coldly in my chest.

She seemed to drink in my words, desperate to believe them, yet there was a flicker of doubt that danced behind her gaze. It was a silent question, one that echoed my own fears of the inevitable collision course I had just set us upon.

The evening wore on, and Ivy moved among our guests like a queen presiding over her court. Her laughter was a melody that filled the room, yet it could not reach the hollow space where my heart beat a rhythm of impending doom. Every toast raised, every hand I shook, was undercut by the knowledge of the threat that lingered just beyond these gilded walls.

I watched Ivy from my peripheral vision, her charm and beauty a beacon in the sea of faces. She was everything I had never known I needed, a contrast to the violence and power that defined my world. Yet here she was, shining amidst the shadows, her love a force that both anchored and terrified me.

As the night drew to a close and our guests departed with wine-stained lips and sated appetites, I felt the magnitude of what lay ahead. Promises made in the soft glow of candlelight would be tested by the harsh light of day. And as Ivy took my arm, leading me away from the remnants of the feast, I knew that no matter the cost, I would move heaven and earth to keep her safe from the ghosts of our pasts.

***

The crystal clinked like a chime of fate as another toast was raised, the sound surrounded me like a fucking noose. I scanned the faces, all smiles and camaraderie, but my chest tightened knowing one of them belonged to a serpent in our midst.

"Dominic, my boy," an older don bellowed, his voice soaked in red wine and mirth, "when will we see you settle down with a Bella Donna? Time isn't your ally forever."

A collective chuckle rippled through the room as eyes turned to Ivy and me. The air grew thick with unspoken words and the weight of expectancy. Under the table, Ivy's hand found my thigh, her touch light yet laden with silent conversation. I caught her gaze, saw the plea for calm there, and squeezed back, the pressure a testament to the storm brewing within.

"Settling down is easy when you find perfection," I replied, the words smooth as the scotch on my tongue, but they left a bitter taste behind.

Later that night, as the moon hung low like a judge over us, Ivy's silhouette stood against the bedroom door, her posture taut with purpose.

"Dominic, this has to end. I can't stand the secrets, the danger. I need to tell my father what's happening," she said, her voice quivering with desperation.

"Tell him?" I spat the words out, anger and fear intertwining. "Ivy, he brought this life upon us. He'll tear everything down, including us. I respect him."

Tears glistened in her eyes like stars caught in her lashes. "You're all I have," she cried, her words slicing through my defenses.

I approached her slowly, feeling the gravity of our bond pulling me closer. "Then don't take me away from you," I whispered, every syllable heavy with the truth of my world. The world I prayed would not consume us both.

* * *

I watched Ivy's retreating figure, her shoulders rigid with the weight of our spat. The door clicked shut behind her, a soft seal on the tension that clung to the air like humidity before a storm. For the first time since she'd entered my life, I let her leave without a word, without a plea. My chest tightened, each breath an effort against the fear that she might not return.

The room felt suffocating without her, the opulence of velvet drapes and gilded frames mocking me with their permanence. I poured myself another drink, amber liquid splashing more out of the glass than into it. The night dragged on, the hands of the clock pushing through molasses as doubts gnawed at my resolve.

It was the ghostly whisper of dawn that finally brought her back.

I heard the faintest shuffle of her feet on the carpet, the tentative push of the door as it opened. She stood there, a silhouette haloed by the soft light of early morning, hesitating.

Then, like a whisper made flesh, she crossed the room and slid into bed beside me. The sheets shifted with her weight, familiar yet foreign in the silence between us.

I remained still as her hand found mine under the covers, the coolness of her skin a balm to the heat of my anxiety.

She didn't speak, and neither did I. Questions loomed, but this moment seemed too fragile for words. Instead, she drew closer, pressing her lips to mine with a tenderness that broke through the chaos, a silent promise that transcended our fears. Her kiss was a vow, unwavering and fierce, sealing us together against the unforgiving world outside our door.

Chapter 12

Ivy

The estate felt like a maze, with twisting hallways that reminded me of my own messy thoughts. Every door seemed to hide a secret or tell a story I wasn't supposed to hear.

I'd wandered aimlessly, driven by a restlessness that wouldn't settle, until I stood before it—a door unlike the others, unassuming yet imposing, as if guarding the threshold to Dominic's soul.

It was locked, naturally.

I traced the cold metal of the doorknob, and I felt the weight of the silence behind it. A paperclip, nothing more than an innocuous piece of metal, transformed under my touch into a key of sorts as I bent and twisted it with a focus I never knew I had. The lock clicked open, a soft betrayal of its purpose, and the door creaked like a secret being pried loose from unwilling lips.

The air inside was stagnant, heavy with dust and the ghosts of decisions past. This was Dominic's old office. Shelves lined with leather-bound books, a desk that bore the scars of time, and shadows clinging to the corners like mourners at a wake. But it was what rested on the mahogany surface that stole my breath—manila folders stacked with precision, each labeled with a meticulous hand.

And one bore my name.

Ivy.

A tremor coursed through my fingers as they hovered over the folder before diving into its contents. Photographs spilled out, images of myself captured in moments I never knew were watched—walking through the park, laughing with friends, existing in a world I thought was mine alone. My heart thrummed a frantic rhythm against my ribcage.

Notes accompanied the pictures, scribbles in Dominic's unmistakable script that detailed mundane aspects of my life with chilling accuracy. Dates, places, observations that read like lines from a stalker's diary. How long had he been doing this? Why?

The room seemed to close in on me, opulence turning oppressive, every luxurious detail a reminder of the man whose shadow I now stood in. I'd been drawn to him, a moth to the flame of his power and enigma. But the flame that once beckoned now threatened to consume me whole.

My heart raced not only with fear but with a dark fascination. What did this discovery make me in the eyes of Dominic Mancini? A mere pawn, an obsession, or something far more dangerous?

The truth lay within these walls, between the lines of his notes. And I needed answers.

* * *

I stormed out of the office, the images and words from those files searing the edges of my consciousness. The marble floors echoed my heavy tread as I sought him out, the man who had somehow etched himself into every facet of my life without my knowledge. Dominic Mancini, the enigma wrapped in tailored suits and smoldering stares, now a specter that haunted the very corners of my past.

I found him where he always seemed to be, in the heart of his domain, surrounded by the quiet hum of power that whispered through the walls of the estate. He was alone, standing before a grand window that overlooked the sprawling gardens, his silhouette commanding yet strangely vulnerable against the fading light.

"Dominic," I said, my voice steady despite the tumult inside me. He turned, his eyes finding mine, and something within them darkened at the sight of the fury I could not contain.

"Ivy," he began, his tone deceptively calm. "What is it?"

"Since I was nineteen?" I threw the accusation like a dagger, watching as it struck closer to home than any physical weapon could. "You've been watching me—stalking me—for years?"

His jaw clenched, and for a moment he was silent, the weight of his confession hanging between us. Then his defenses fell, and the truth poured out, raw and unadorned. "Yes," he admitted, his voice rough with an emotion I couldn't place. "But I never meant for this...until now."

The air sucked out of the room, leaving a vacuum where my controlled rage had been. In its place, a wild, untamed fury unfurled, and without thought, my hand lashed out, connecting sharply with his cheek. The sound cracked through the silence of the room, a fitting punctuation to the chaos he'd wrought.

He barely moved, absorbing the blow as if it were just a caress. But when he looked at me again, there was a fire in his eyes that matched the one burning through my veins.

"God, Ivy..." His voice was a low growl, filled with a torment I knew mirrored my own.

Impulse overrode reason, and I stepped into him, eliminating the space that divided our worlds. My lips crashed against his with a ferocity that stole my breath, the impact resonating through me. "You were mine before I ever knew it," I whispered against his mouth, the words tasting of a bitter truth that we both recognized.

In that moment, the lines blurred, the years of clandestine observation and the shock of discovery melding into a singular point of connection. There was no denying the magnetic pull that brought us here, to this precipice of desire and darkness. And as our kiss deepened, so did the understanding that this was no longer just about possession or control.

It was about the collision of two fates, inevitably entwined.

* * *

I clawed at the fabric of Dominic's shirt, buttons scattering like shrapnel as we stumbled toward the bed. His hands were all over my curves, a storm that raged against my skin, leaving trails of heat in its wake. The mattress welcomed us with a silent thud, our bodies entwined in a chaos of limbs and sheets.

"Dominic," I gasped, caught between anger and aching need. My fingers raked through his hair, pulling him closer until there was no space for secrets, no room for lies—just the raw intensity of our breaths mingling in the charged air.

"Tell me you want this," he demanded, voice rough with emotion. But it wasn't just lust that weighed down his words—it was something deeper, a fear that resonated in his touch.

"More than my next breath," I confessed, and it was true. Despite the madness, despite knowing too much and too little, my body sang with the truth of it.

We moved together, a frenetic dance fueled by rage and obsession. There was relief, too, in acknowledging the pull between us, in surrendering to it fully. Every gasp and moan wrote a new chapter in our twisted story, each movement a promise of more—more pleasure, more pain, more everything.

In the aftermath, as our breathing slowed and the world narrowed to the rise and fall of his chest against mine, Dominic's voice broke the silence. It was barely above a whisper, but it cut through the haze like a knife.

"Ivy, I'm scared."

My heart skidded to a halt. "Of what?" Even as I asked, I feared the answer.

"Not dying," he murmured, tracing the line of my jaw with a tenderness that contrasted starkly with the brutality of our coupling. "But of losing you."

The vulnerability in those words startled me, a crack in the armor of the most powerful man I'd ever known. And in that moment, I saw him—not the mafia boss, not the shadow that had haunted my steps—but Dominic, the man who feared as fiercely as he loved.

"Then don't let go," I whispered back, sealing the vow with a kiss that tasted of salt and sin. And for the first time since I'd been thrust into this gilded cage, I wondered if maybe—just maybe—I didn't want to escape after all.

* * *

Dominic's fingers stilled on my skin, his eyes searching mine in the dim afterglow. The air between us was thick with unspoken truths, each one heavier than the last. His confession lingered, a ghost that neither of us could exorcise.

"Then don't," I said softly, the weight of my own admission settling into the room like a tangible presence. It was a plea, a challenge, a tether thrown across the chasm that divided our worlds. In those three words, I gave voice to something raw and new—something perilous and precious.

He pulled me closer, as if he could shield us both from the reality we faced. Our silence was filled with the gravity of what went unsaid, but it was enough. It had to be.

Outside, the night held its breath, the sprawling estate a kingdom of shadows under the watchful gaze of the moon. Dante stood before an array of screens, his expression unreadable as he monitored every corner, every hidden alcove. He took in the tangled limbs, the tender brutality of our embrace, and nodded to himself. The lines around his eyes deepened, not with anger or surprise, but with a solemn understanding.

He knew. The way Dominic clung to me, the desperation with which I clung back—Dante understood the stakes of the game that was no longer just a game. And in that moment, with the flicker of screens casting an eerie glow upon his stoic face, Dante became the silent guardian of a secret that was never meant to be kept.

Chapter 13

Ivy

The night was a cloak, and under its cover, Dante slunk through the shadows towards the old villa where Ivy's father held court. His heart throbbed against his chest, a traitor to the silence he tried to maintain. But it wasn't the stealth that pained him; it was the betrayal that weighed on his conscience like lead.

I took a deep breath, feeling the crisp air fill my lungs as I watched from the window of Dominic's estate. The moonlight caressed the marble floors, the surrounding opulence a stark contrast to the turmoil within. I was draped in one of Dominic's shirts the fabric hanging loose over my shoulders. My feet were bare, toes curling against the cold stone, unaware of the storm that was about to break.

The door burst open with a violence that echoed through the grand hallways, jolting me from my reverie. I stumbled back, my heart leapfrogging to my throat.

There stood my father, his face contorted with rage, his body emanating a fury that could singe the very air around us.

"Father?" I choked out, my voice barely a whisper against the tidal wave of his wrath. He looked at me then, his eyes raking over my disheveled appearance, taking in every detail that marked me not as his daughter but as an entity intertwined with the man he despised.

"Is this how I find you? In his clothes?" His words were bullets, and they hit their target, shattering the last vestige of calm I had clung to.

I felt so small standing there, caught between the life I had known and the one I was stepping into—a no-man's-land that now seemed more treacherous than ever.

* * *

The air crackled with a dangerous energy, the sound of my father's roar slicing through the silence like a blade. Father moved swift punching Dominic's jaw in a forceful shove that made a sickening thud against the backdrop of ornate walls and looming portraits. The room spun as I threw myself into the fray, my voice lost in the cacophony.

"Stop it!" I screamed, but it sounded weak even to my own ears. My hands pressed against my father's chest, the fabric of his shirt bunching under my desperate grip. "Please, just stop!"

Dominic steadied himself, his dark eyes smoldering coals of intensity as he straightened to his full height. He didn't flinch at my father's next shout, nor did he waver under the weight of his accusatory glare. The air between them was thick with unspoken history.

"I didn't seduce her," Dominic said, his voice low and unwavering, every syllable dripping with solemn reverence. "I worshipped her."

Holy freaking hell—

The declaration hung heavy in the room, a sacred truth cloaked in defiance. I could feel the weight of his gaze, the depth of his words, and something within me shifted irrevocably. In that moment, Dominic stood not as a menacing figure of power but as a man laid bare, his devotion a stark contrast to the chaos swirling around us.

"Worshipped her?" Father retorted.

* * *

Rage contorted my father's face into a mask I hardly recognized. His voice was a whip crack in the silence that followed Dominic's brazen confession.

"I love him, father!" I cried out.

"Are you hearing yourself, Ivy?" he spat out my name like it was a curse. "You're being a fool!"

His words struck me, but I squared my shoulders, refusing to shrink away. The plush carpet beneath my bare feet felt like treacherous ground, yet I stood my ground. I met his glare with a steadiness I didn't feel.

"I am no fool, and certainly not your little girl anymore," I replied, my voice steady despite the maelstrom of emotions inside me. "This is my choice."

The words hung between us, a declaration of independence I could never retract. His eyes searched mine, looking for the daughter he thought he knew, the one who would bow to his will.

"Choice?" He laughed bitterly, the sound slicing through the tension-thick air. "This...

alliance was built on more than your whims, Ivy. Remember our family, our legacy."

He turned on Dominic, a predator cornering its prey. "If you think I'll stand by and watch you destroy everything we've worked for, you are gravely mistaken."

Dominic's response was as cold as the marble statues that adorned the hallways. "Threaten the alliance if you must," he said, every word a nail sealing an unseen coffin. "But know this - then you've already ended us all."

His statement fell swift and final. It was a prophecy of doom wrapped in certainty, a grim reminder that our fates were intertwined with a bond stronger and more perilous than any of us had imagined. My heart pounded a frenzied beat, knowing that whatever came next, the world we knew was precariously balanced on the edge of a knife.

* * *

The door slammed with a violence that echoed through the cavernous halls of Dominic's estate, a definitive punctuation to my father's fury. I stood motionless for a fraction of a second, the tremors of his departure rattling through my bones before my knees gave way. I crumbled, a puppet with its strings cut, the cold floor against my bare feet.

Tears cascaded down my cheeks, unbidden and unrestrained, as sobs wracked my frame. I was dimly aware of the world tilting, the opulent room spinning, when strong arms enveloped me. Dominic. His embrace was an anchor in the storm, yet there was no comfort in the rigid set of his jaw or the icy fire in his eyes.

Dominic brushed a stray lock of hair from my tear-stained face, his touch surprisingly gentle for a man carved from stone. He held me close, but there was a distance in his gaze, as if he were looking past me, into a future painted with uncertainty.

"This is war now," Dominic's voice was a murmur, a low growl that seemed to reverberate through my very soul. He meant it, every syllable soaked in a lethal calm that belied the chaos unfurling around us.

I clung to him, my heart hammering, as the weight of his words settled over me. War. Not just a clash of wills or a battle of egos, but a tangible, destructive force that could ravage everything we knew. My tears slowed, not out of relief, but from the numbing realization that we had crossed a line from which there was no return.

Chapter 14

Ivy

Days later

I felt it before I heard it—the subtle shift in the room, the way the air grew colder, as if the very breath of loyalty had been sucked out. Whispers crept like tendrils of fog through the opulent halls of Dominic's mansion, carrying with them a scent of betrayal. The men who once stood by his side, eyes gleaming with unwavering commitment, now averted their gazes, their postures stiff with uncertainty.

"Dominic," I murmured, my voice barely rising above the hushed tones that filled the grand chamber. "Something's wrong."

He didn't look at me, his eyes scanning the room like a predator sensing the weakening of its pack. His grip on the city, something I'd thought unshakable, trembled on the precipice of dissent.

"Let me help," I pleaded, taking a step toward him. The fine silk of my dress whispered against my legs, an incongruent sound amidst the silent chaos.

"Stay out of this, Ivy," he said, his voice low, a dangerous edge to each word. "This isn't your fight."

"It is when it affects us," I shot back, frustration simmering within. I couldn't stand being a decorative piece in his world, not when everything was falling to pieces around us. "Maybe if I talk to my father—"

"No." The command sliced through the space between us. "You are not to see him. That's final."

The finality in his tone freaking stung, a stark contrast to the warm man who'd once let his guard down only for me. Now, it seemed, even I could not reach him. My heart raced, thoughts scattered like leaves in a storm. I wanted to fix this, to mend the cracks before they splintered into irreparable rifts, but Dominic's fortress had no doors open to me.

"Dominic, please." My plea hung in the air, unanswered. He turned away, his silhouette rigid against the fading light filtering through the tall windows.

Defeat settled heavy in my chest as I watched the allies, once close as brothers, slip like shadows from the room. Alone in the center stood Dominic, his empire trembling, and I, forbidden to do anything but watch it crumble.

* * *

I slipped through the shadows, a ghost in my life. The chill of the night air couldn't compare to the frost inside Dominic's mansion. With each step away from that gilded cage, my heart pounded an erratic rhythm, half terror, half thrill. I was doing this—breaking Dominic's one decree. But the city's whispers had become screams, and I couldn't silence them with ignorance.

The café was an island of neutrality amidst the turbulent sea of our families' histories. Its windows were fogged, a veil for the secrets it kept. I pushed through the door, the jingle of the bell announcing my betrayal.

There he sat, my father, wrapped in the anonymity of a corner booth. His eyes, mirrors of my own, found me instantly. They were clouded with storms of anger, disappointment, resignation.

"Ivy," he greeted, his voice a relic of softer times.

"Father." My tongue felt heavy with the weight of that word.

We danced around pleasantries as if they could bandage the wounds between us. The scent of coffee and pastries fought against the bitterness in the air.

"Please," I began, my hands clenched in my lap, "we must fix this. There has to be some peace we can broker."

"Peace?" He scoffed, the sound cutting deep. "Do you understand what you've done? You've bound yourself to him, to Dominic, and now my flesh and blood are my undoing."

"Father, I—I didn't mean—" My words crumbled like the sugar cubes beside my untouched coffee.

"Didn't mean to ruin me?" His accusation was a whip, each syllable a lash that stripped away my resolve.

"Dominic's world is falling apart," I whispered, desperation seeping into my voice. "If we don't do something—"

"Let it fall!" His fist hit the table, a punctuation mark ending all debate. "You chose your side the moment you left my house. You are no longer my concern."

I looked at the man before me, searching for a trace of the father I used to idolize. All I found was a stranger wearing his skin, a stranger who'd disowned me as easily as shedding an old coat.

"Then there's nothing more to say," I said, my voice a hollow echo of the girl I once was.

Rising from the booth, I walked out, leaving behind the warmth of the café for the biting cold outside. I walked out broken, shards of my heart littering the path back to a home that was no sanctuary, to a man whose love was a fortress I could neither escape nor defend.

* * *

Dominic's silence was a thunderous roar, echoing through the cavernous halls of our home. I felt it before I saw him, standing in the doorway, the fading light casting long shadows over his brooding figure. There was no need for words; his eyes said it all. He knew where I had been.

"Next time, I'll burn the city to keep you here," he said, voice low and devoid of its usual fiery command. It wasn't a shout that could shake the walls—it was a promise whispered like a curse, one that chilled me more than any tempest howling outside our windows.

I couldn't muster a reply. The weight of my betrayal, heavy as lead, settled in my chest, making it hard to breathe. His presence receded, footsteps silent on the thick carpet, leaving me to standalone amidst the opulence that felt more like a gilded cage with every passing second.

For two days, the house turned into a glacier. The air between us crackled with cold, unspoken fury. We moved like specters through the vast rooms, our encounters brief and wordless, as if even the slightest utterance would shatter the fragile veneer of calm.

I took refuge in the loneliness of our bed, now an icy expanse where once there had been warmth. The silk sheets, smooth against my skin, provided no comfort as I curled up on my side, hugging my knees, willing sleep to claim me and freeze out the tumultuous emotions swirling within.

Each night dragged into eternity, the darkness punctuated by the distant chime of the grandfather clock, marking the hours with relentless precision. And each chime was a reminder of the widening rift, a crescendo building to a climax that I dreaded yet yearned for. My heart ached for something, anything, that would melt the frost that had settled over us. But the flames of our passion, once so fierce they threatened to consume us both, now seemed like embers struggling to stay alight.

When at last dawn painted the sky with strokes of pink and gold, the beauty of the new day felt like mockery. In a house where silence reigned supreme, where every glance was laden with accusations and remorse, what place was there for the softness of morning light?

As I rose from the bed, the absence of his warmth beside me was a stark reminder of the distance that had grown between us. A divide that seemed as insurmountable as the walls of this grand mausoleum we called home.

* * *

The stillness of the mansion was a freaking lie, a facade as deceptive as our silence. I roamed the halls like a specter, my footsteps muffled by the thick carpets that lined the floors, every creak of the old wood beneath them a whisper of unrest. The portraits on the walls, ancestors of a crime dynasty, watched with indifferent eyes, their painted smirks hinting at secrets that would send lesser souls to their knees.

I could feel him before I saw him, the weight of his presence more oppressive than the gilded chandeliers that hung overhead. Dominic, the man who held my life in his hands, who commanded respect and fear in equal measure. He found me in the sunroom, the slanted rays of light casting long shadows across the space that felt neither here nor there, much like us.

His steps were silent but purposeful, closing the distance between us with a determination that made my heart hammer against the cage of my ribs. When he reached me, he didn't speak. Instead, he knelt before me, the don of the underworld looking up with a vulnerability that shattered the last defenses around my heart.

"I'm losing you," he said, voice barely above a whisper, yet it filled the room, reverberated against the walls, and settled heavy on my shoulders.

The sight of him, this formidable man brought to his knees, wrenched a sob from my chest. My hands trembled as I reached out to touch his face, tracing the lines of worry that had etched themselves into his skin these past days. Everything within me wanted to pull him close, to erase the anguish that marred his features, but the hurt was too raw, the betrayal too deep.

"Then fight for me," I whispered back, my plea hanging between us like a prayer. It was a challenge, a gauntlet thrown at his feet, asking him to prove that we were worth more than the power struggles and the dark whispers that threatened to engulf us.

For a moment, he just looked at me, his gaze searching mine, as if trying to find the girl he'd once known in the eyes of the woman before him. And then, as if a switch had been flipped, the don rose to his feet, his resolve hardening like steel. He would fight. Not with guns or threats, but with the ferocity of a man who refused to lose the only light in his darkness.

He reached for me, wrapping his arms around me with a finesse that belied his strength, pulling me into the storm that raged within him. We stood there, in the fragmented light of the fading day, two souls caught in the crossfire of love and war, ready to rise from the ashes or burn together in the inferno of our own making.

Chapter 15

Dominic

I reached for the encrypted phone line, the one that connected me to a world I was bred to rule but desperate to escape. I tapped out a message that could seal my fate, or maybe just postpone the reckoning. "One meeting. Neutral ground," I typed, my heart punching against my chest like it wanted out.

"Agreed. But this ain't a truce, boy," came the reply not moments later. The screen glowed with the venom of a man who had loved and lost too much, including his daughter's loyalty.

I pocketed the device and turned to find Ivy, her face a pale canvas of worry, eyes wide and haunted. She was a striking contrast in the dim light of our hideout—a place that felt more like a tomb every day. "Dominic, please," she whispered, her voice barely there yet slicing through me sharper than any blade.

"I have to go, Ivy," I said, the truth tasting bitter. She looked like a prayer in that moment, all soft edges and silent pleas.

"Alone?" Her voice cracked on the word, a fracture spreading across the ice we were both standing on.

"Alone."

She reached out, her hand trembling as it found mine, her touch anchoring me to the here and now. I brought her fingers to my lips, reverence mingling with the ever-present fear that clung to our shadows.

"Come back to me," she breathed, a command wrapped in a beg.

I cupped her face, my thumb tracing the line of her jaw, memorizing the feel of her skin against the roughness of my own. I kissed her with a desperation I couldn't afford to show, but couldn't contain either. It was a kiss filled with every unspoken promise and unsaid goodbye, a meeting of souls at the crossroad of hell.

"Always," I vowed against her lips, tasting the salt of her tears.

Then I stepped away, leaving warmth for cold, certainty for chaos. I left part of myself with her in that room, hoping I'd be whole enough to reclaim it when the night was over.

* * *

The door to the old warehouse groaned on its hinges as I pushed it open, stepping into a cavernous space where shadows clung stubbornly to the walls. My footsteps echoed, a solitary drumbeat heralding my entrance into a lion's den. His territory. Ivy's father waited in the center, a king in his court of darkness.

"Dominic," he greeted me, his voice a gravelly chord that resonated with hostility.

"Mr. Donati," I replied, my tone icy politeness wrapped around an iron core of resolve. I stopped a few paces away, close enough to see the lines etched deeply into his face, far enough to keep from striking distance.

"Let's not pretend this is a social call," he sneered, his eyes narrowing.

I remained stoic, though each word he spat felt like a gut punch. "I'm here for Ivy."

"Ah, my daughter," he said, spitting out the words like they left a bitter aftertaste. "You've got some nerve showing your face after what you've done."

"Done? You mean falling in love with her?" I challenged, my voice steady despite the tempest raging inside me.

"Corrupting her, you mean," he shot back. "Dragging her into your filthy world."

"Filthy world?" It was my turn to laugh, the sound hollow and mirthless. "It seems we share more than just the city's underbelly, Mr. Donati."

Accusations continued to fly between us, sharper than shrapnel. He blamed me for every sin under the sun, painting me as a monster in a story where he saw himself as the hero. But heroes don't lock up their daughters, don't trade them like chess pieces in power plays. He asked why a man who was supposed to protect his daughter would dishonor his vow by sleeping with her. He said I was no longer worthy.

I took a deep breath and exhaled.

"Enough!" I finally bellowed, my patience threadbare. "If me walking away from all of this is what it takes to keep her safe, then so be it. I'll leave it all behind."

His eyes searched mine, looking for the lie, the weakness. But there was nothing but unwavering truth staring back at him. "You'd give up your empire for her?" he asked, skepticism lacing his inquiry.

"Without a second thought," I affirmed, my heart pounding with the sincerity of my declaration.

He stared at me, a long hard gaze that seemed to cut through to my soul. Then, with a cold chuckle, he leaned back slightly. "Bravo, Dominic. But do you honestly think I believe you'd ever walk away from your precious control?"

In that moment, his doubt stung, the sting of it searing through the facade of indifference I tried to maintain. But it was a pain I accepted as the cost of this war—a war I fought for love, not territory.

"Believe what you want," I replied, my voice quiet but firm. "But know this: Ivy's safety comes first."

He regarded me with a hard, unreadable expression, and for a split second, I wondered if perhaps we understood each other better than we cared to admit.

* * *

The silence in the air thickened, heavy with the weight of unspoken threats and the shadow of impending loss. I felt it cling to my skin, a tangible reminder that this was no ordinary negotiation. It was a reckoning between two worlds that should never have collided.

"Fine," I said, my voice low, carrying across the expanse of the ornate room designed for intimidation. "She chose me. You either accept it—or you lose her."

I watched him closely, saw the muscle in his jaw twitch, a subtle betrayal of the storm brewing within. His eyes, so much like Ivy's in their piercing intensity, bore into me. In them, I saw the struggle—the love of a father warring with the pride of a man who had never been challenged.

There was a long silence. The kind that screamed louder than any words could. It stretched on, each second a defiant standoff that refused to break under the sheer force of wills colliding.

Then, from the depths of that silence, he spoke, his voice barely above a whisper, yet it cut through the tension like the sharpest blade. "I see her in you. That's what scares me."

His admission hung in the air, raw and revealing. And in that moment, I understood that our battle was not just for power or dominance—it was a fight for the very thing that made us human. Love. Fear. The fragile threads that bound us all.

As I stood there, absorbing the impact of his words, I realized that perhaps there was more of him in me than I had ever cared to admit. But unlike him, I would not let fear dictate my future. Not with Ivy.

* * *

I stood, the chill of the room closing in around me like a shroud. Ivy's father held my gaze, his expression carved from stone. Neither of us moved to bridge the distance with the customary shake of hands—the mafia's gesture of concluded deals and grudging respect. It remained unspoken, yet the air shifted, the weight of mutual enmity lifting just enough to let in a sliver of truce. The war was over, hanging by the thinnest thread.

I turned on my heel, the echo of my footsteps a lonely drumbeat against the grandeur of the cold, high-ceilinged room. My hand felt the absence of another; it was an ache, a hollow yearning for the warmth that came with Ivy's touch.

Outside, the night had blanketed the city, stars hidden behind the light pollution like secrets cloaked in darkness. I made my way through the quiet streets, each step heavy with thoughts of what had transpired. The encounter with her father would change things, set us on a path that neither of us could predict. Uncertainty gnawed at me, but the fire that Ivy ignited in my soul burned away the worst of my doubts.

When I reached our sanctuary, the door opened before I could knock, as if she sensed my presence. Ivy stood there, her eyes wide and luminous in the dim light. Relief flooded her features when she saw me, a silent testament to the hours of worry that had etched lines into her perfect face. She threw herself into my arms, her body shaking with silent sobs.

"We're not safe," I admitted, holding her tight against me. The truth tasted bitter, but it needed to be told. "But we're together." Her tears soaked into my shirt, each drop a promise that I would keep her close, protect her against the chaos that swirled just beyond our haven.

In the darkness of our refuge, with her nestled against my chest, the world outside melted away. There, in the forced proximity that had become our cocoon, we found the courage to face whatever lay ahead. Together.

Chapter 16

Ivy

Weeks later.

Here I was, in love Dominic Mancini? It was freaking surreal.

I twisted the gold band on my finger, a nervous habit I'd picked up since wearing Dominic's ring. The car rolled to a stop outside the familiar iron gates, their ornate swirls a stark contrast to the heaviness in my chest. I stepped out, each step was a choice—a choice to face my past.

"Ten minutes," the driver said, his voice a low rumble meant for intimidation. Dominic's reluctant permission hung in the air, thick and unyielding.

"Understood," I replied, not daring to glance at his shadowed figure in the rearview mirror.

The door to my childhood home opened with a creak that sounded like a mournful sigh. My father sat in the dimly lit parlor, his once imposing figure now shrunken into the depths of an overstuffed armchair. Age hadn't just touched him; it had taken residence in the creases of his face.

"Hello, Father," I said, my voice barely above a whisper.

"Isabella my baby," he corrected automatically, his eyes narrowing as if he could rewrite my identity with a single word.

"Ivy," I insisted gently. "It's Ivy now."

Silence stretched between us, taut and fragile. He looked away first, his gaze settling on the dying embers in the fireplace.

"Dominic's doing well, then?" he asked, his tone carefully neutral.

"Better than you'd wish," I admitted, sitting on the edge of the sofa, my hands clasped to stop them from shaking.

We spoke of inconsequential things—weather, health, the state of the garden. Each sentence was a tentative step across a chasm of years filled with rebellion and resentment. With every careful word, a sliver of understanding passed between us, hinting at a bridge that could be built with time and forgiveness.

Before leaving, I slipped an envelope onto the mahogany coffee table, its creamy surface stark against the dark wood. Inside, words poured from my heart, hopeful and raw.

"Read this when I'm gone," I said, my eyes meeting his momentarily. "It's about... the future."

He nodded once, a terse dip of his head that acknowledged the weight of what I left behind. I turned and walked away, the door closing with a soft click that seemed to echo louder than any slammed door of my teenage years.

Outside, I took a deep breath, the night air crisp and clear. I imagined a day, maybe not too far off, when those gates would open not to let me out, but to welcome us both in. A day when my father would watch me walk down an aisle, perhaps even smile as I promised forever to a man he never chose for me, but one I chose for myself.

"Time to go back," the driver called out, his voice a reminder of the world I was returning to—one of unspoken rules and hidden daggers.

As we drove away, the house faded into the darkness.

I sighed thinking, wow, a closed chapter, yet holding the promise of a new beginning, one penned by my hand.

***

I stepped out of the vehicle. The estate loomed before me, its grandeur overshadowed by the weight of the night's revelations. I had left a piece of myself in that house, a letter that held more hope than I'd allowed myself to feel in years.

A shiver ran down my spine, not from the chill in the air but from the sensation of being watched. My eyes searched the shadows until they landed on him, Dominic, standing at a respectful distance.

He leaned against the black sedan, arms crossed over his chest, his gaze fixed on me with an intensity that felt like a physical touch. It was as if he could see through every defense I'd ever constructed, laying bare the vulnerability I fought so hard to conceal.

In that moment, there was nothing else—no family feuds, no criminal empires—just Dominic and me, and the silent understanding that we were together by more than circumstance. Despite the chaos that seemed to follow us, he was still mine, steadfast and unwavering. And I marveled at it. That someone like Dominic, forged in darkness and danger, would choose to stand by me, when the world had given us every reason to let go.

"Come," he said, his voice low and inviting. "Tonight, we forget about all of it."

We walked hand in hand towards the garden where moonlight danced across the meticulously trimmed hedges and the scent of blooming roses lingered in the air. There was a surreal quality to it, this oasis of peace amidst a life of constant vigilance. As we stepped onto the soft grass, I realized Dominic had planned this, a rare night off—a reprieve from our reality.

He took me into his arms, and we swayed to a music only we could hear, our bodies moving together in perfect harmony. The moon hung heavy above us, casting us in its silver glow, and for once, there were no guns tucked into holsters, no guards with watchful eyes scanning for threats. Just us, Ivy and Dominic, two people finding solace in each other's embrace.

My head rested against his chest, and I could hear the steady beat of his heart, a rhythm that calmed the storm within me. We danced like that for what felt like hours, lost in a world where time didn't exist, where the past and future were just words without meaning.

As we turned beneath the celestial canvas, I closed my eyes, allowing myself to be consumed by the feeling of absolute freedom. Tonight, I wasn't running, wasn't hiding—I was just a girl in the arms of the man she loved, surrounded by beauty that whispered promises of what could be.

And in the quiet garden, I believed that maybe, just maybe, we could have it all.

***

I stepped back from Dominic, our dance slowing to an end, and looked up into his eyes, searching. The night was ours, but I knew that the dawn would bring back the weight of the world we lived in, heavy on his shoulders.

"Dominic," I began, my voice barely above a whisper, "what do you want next?"

His gaze held mine, deep and fathomless, like the night sky above us. He was a man carved from the shadows of power and danger, yet in this stolen moment, he seemed as vulnerable as I had ever seen him.

"A life where I don't have to look over my shoulder," he confessed, the words falling between us like a vow.

The longing in his voice pierced through me, echoing the silent prayers I'd often whispered into the darkness. We were bound by a love that was as fierce as it was unexpected, born from a world where trust was the most expensive commodity.

"Then let's build it," I said, a fierce determination rising within me. I reached for his hand, entwining our fingers as if to weave together the future I envisioned for us—a future free from the constant threat that lurked at the edge of our existence.

Dominic's lips found mine in a kiss that sealed our pact, passionate and promising. It was a kiss that spoke of beginnings rather than endings, of hope instead of fear. In his embrace, I could feel the contours of a different life taking shape—one where each day wasn't shadowed by the sins of our past.

As he kissed me like I was his future, I realized we were not just surviving; we were transcending the legacy of blood and betrayal that had brought us together. In that perfect, fragile moment, we were building something new, something ours, out of the darkness that had always defined us.

***

The night wrapped around us like a silken shroud, the air thick with the scent of jasmine from the garden below. I nestled into Dominic's arms, our earlier dance under the moonlight still a lingering warmth on my skin. The garden had been a sanctuary, free from the pervasive gaze of guards and the silent threat of guns.

In his embrace, the world seemed to fall away. My heartbeat slowed to match the rhythm of his chest, rising and falling. It was in this quiet space that I felt the truth of our earlier promise settling over me, a blanket woven from threads of hope and determination. For the first time since the chaos began, I wasn't plotting an escape.

I was just Ivy, and he was just Dominic, two souls finding solace in the stillness.

My eyelids fluttered shut, heavy with the exhaustion of a day spent balancing on the precipice between past pain and future dreams. His fingers traced idle patterns on my back, soothing the last remnants of tension until they ebbed away like the tide. I surrendered to sleep, lulled by the steady thump of his heart—a lullaby more potent than any whispered words.

Dawn broke with a soft glow, creeping through the curtains as if hesitant to disturb the peace we'd found. It was the shrill ring of a phone that shattered the silence, wrenching Dominic from the depths of slumber before the sun could lay claim to the day.

His body tensed as he reached for the device, every muscle coiled like a spring. The old instincts, never far from the surface, flared to life in his eyes as he glanced at the screen. I watched through half-closed lids, a silent observer caught between rest and wakefulness.

"Si," he answered in a hushed tone, a stark contrast to the burgeoning light.

A pause hung in the air, dense with unspoken words. Dominic listened more than he spoke, his responses terse nods and curt affirmations. But as the call drew to a close, something shifted in his posture. A release, subtle but unmistakable, as if invisible chains were falling away one by one.

He ended the call, the finality in the click echoing softly in the room. Dominic turned to me, the early rays of sunlight painting golden streaks across his face. There was a clarity in his gaze, a calm that hadn't been there before.

"Your father," he began, his voice a low rumble that vibrated against my cheek. "He didn't say it in so many words, but... he's given his blessing."

That simple declaration felt like a keystone sliding into place in the archway of our lives. Unspoken but undeniable, it was a gift of freedom—the kind that only family can bestow. As

I gazed up at him, the man who had become both my haven and my heart, I knew we crossed an invisible threshold. No longer bound by the specters of our past, we stood at the cusp of a new beginning—one we would build together, brick by hard-fought brick.

Chapter 17

Dominic

"She deserves a bigger ring!" I whispered under my breath. "No more pretending she's going to be mine fully."

I walked through the narrow streets that twisted like the alleys of my mind, each turn laden with a new decision.

The air was brisk, carrying the scent of the sea, and it seemed to push me forward.

I found myself standing in front of an old jeweler's shop, its window display subtle under the shadowy eaves.

The door chimed as I entered, a sound too delicate for the world I came from. Inside, glass cases gleamed under muted lighting, each holding promises of forever. But I wasn't looking for forever in the shine or the sparkle. I needed something solid, something that could withstand the storms. Like Ivy.

"Can I help you find something?" The shopkeeper's voice was smooth, accustomed to persuasion. But I wasn't a man to be swayed.

"I need a ring," I said. My gaze landed on one that seemed to whisper her name. It wasn't encrusted with diamonds or wrought with intricate designs. It was platinum, strong, its edges sharp, a band that knew its purpose. Just like Ivy. Unyielding yet embracing. I pointed. "That one."

"Ah, a discerning choice," he noted, slipping the ring from the velvet. It felt heavy, significant in my palm.

"Wrap it up," I told him, my voice betraying none of the turbulence inside.

At home, I tucked the small box away, hidden within the confines of my wardrobe. Ivy had always been perceptive, and lately, she'd been watching me with those eyes that saw too much. I could feel her curiosity like a physical touch, but she respected the silences that grew between us. She knew when to probe and when to let the sleeping demons lie.

I planned the proposal in the quiet hours of dawn when the world was nothing but hushed tones and possibilities. In my study, amidst ledgers and the faint smell of leather and gun oil, I mapped out every detail. The right words, the right moment. I wanted to strip away the shadows that clung to my life and offer her clarity, a promise etched in the steel of my resolve.

She must have sensed the shift, the careful orchestration behind my casual facade. Yet she held her tongue, moving through our days with that graceful patience that always seemed to say, "When you're ready, I'm here." And I loved her all the more for it. She was the still point in my chaotic world, the silent strength in my relentless storm.

It was coming, the bending of my knee, the offering of a ring – not just a piece of metal, but everything I was and hoped to be. For her. Only for her.

* * *

The cold steel of the gun pressed lightly against my side was a constant reminder of the life I'd woven around myself, a tapestry of danger and duty. That morning, the weight felt heavier, like it knew the significance of what was to come. As I paced the length of my office, the ring in my pocket was a burning presence, its simplicity a stark contrast to the ornate opulence that surrounded me.

A knock at the door snapped my focus back to the present. I straightened my jacket as Dante stepped into the room, his eyes searching mine for any hint of the old anger. His return wasn't unexpected; loyalties in our world were like tides, ebbing and flowing with the moon's pull. But this time, he came not as an adversary but as an ally seeking absolution.

"Dominic," he started, his voice betraying nothing of the betrayal we'd once bled over, "I'm here to make peace. To swear fealty again."

His words hung in the air, thick with history and unsaid promises. The easy thing would have been to dismiss him, to hold on to past grudges like the many weapons hidden throughout the room. But Ivy's influence ran deep, her quiet strength reminding me that forgiveness was a power all its own.

"Your loyalty is noted," I said, my tone measured, betraying none of the turmoil beneath. "But actions speak louder than oaths, Dante. Remember that."

He nodded, understanding the weight of my warning, the unspoken threat that laced each syllable. Our shared past, rife with conflict and camaraderie, allowed for no illusions between us. With a last nod, he turned and left, leaving me alone with the ghosts of what had been and the hope of what was yet to come.

Later, as the sun dipped low, casting long shadows across the city, I found myself leading Ivy down to the docks. The salty tang of the sea mingled with the pungent odor of fish and diesel, a stark contrast to the world she'd grown accustomed to by my side. But it was here, amidst the cacophony of seagulls and ship horns, where I'd first seen her as more than just a child—where the woman she'd become had rendered me speechless.

"Dominic, why are we here?" Ivy's voice was a melody against the backdrop of crashing waves and creaking wood.

"Because this is where it all began," I replied, watching as realization dawned in her clear, discerning eyes.

Her hand found mine, warm and reassuring, as we walked along the pier. The boats bobbed gently in the water, their hulls scraping softly against the worn planks. This was where I'd stood years ago, where the innocence of youth had fallen away, and the gravity of a life intertwined with hers had taken root.

"Here," I said simply, stopping at the edge of the dock, the last fingers of daylight dancing across the horizon. "This is where I saw you, really saw you, and knew that nothing would ever be the same."

She looked out across the water, her eyes reflecting the hues of the twilight sky. In this place stripped of pretense, with only the chorus of the sea to bear witness, I was ready to lay bare my soul and bind it to hers.

* * *

I released a breath I didn't realize I'd been holding, the salt air filling my lungs as the echoes of a life spent in shadows clung to the fringes of my thoughts. The docks were empty now, save for Ivy and me, our footsteps the only sound over the whisper of the tide.

"Dominic?" Her voice was laced with curiosity and something else—anticipation, maybe. "What is it?"

I turned to face her, watched the way the dying light played across her features, casting shadows that only made her seem more radiant. This wasn't just the girl I'd protected; this was the woman who'd stormed the fortress around my heart without even trying.

"I've lived a life of half-truths, Ivy," I started, my voice steady despite the turmoil raging within. "But with you, I want everything laid bare." My hands shook slightly as I reached into my jacket pocket, feeling the cool metal of the ring against my fingertips. It was a solid thing, unpretentious but undeniable—like her.

Her eyes widened as she took in my resolve, the gravity of the moment rooting her to the spot. "Dominic..."

"Since the day I saw you here, really saw you, you've haunted me," I confessed, the words tumbling out like they'd been caged for too long. "You deserve a truth untainted by the dark corners of my world."

So I told her everything—the deals made in desperation, the alliances forged and broken, the weight of a legacy I never asked for but couldn't escape. And when I spoke of Dante, his betrayal, and his return, it was with the clarity of someone who's survived the storm and come out on the other side.

"Dominic..." she whispered again, a plea or a prayer. I couldn't tell.

"Shh," I hushed her gently, dropping to one knee on the rough planks, the ring now clenched in my hand. "Ivy, I—"

"Yes."

The word was a gunshot in the silence, immediate and resounding. She didn't need my promises; she was already mine, as I was hers. In an instant, she was in my arms, her lips finding mine with a fervor that spoke of every unsaid word between us.

We kissed amidst the sanctuary of the docks, the taste of salt on our tongues, the rest of the world fading into insignificance. Nothing else mattered—no past, no future—just the two of us, bound by a promise as enduring as the sea.

* * *

The night wrapped around us like a cloak as we walked back from the docks, my hand clasped in Ivy's. The cool breeze carried the scent of brine and the distant echo of foghorns, a lullaby for the city that never truly slept.

Back at my penthouse, with its towering view of the skyline that felt both like a kingdom and a cage, I poured us each a glass of wine. She took hers with a smile, the kind that always seemed to see right through me. We settled on the sofa, her head finding its place against my shoulder. Silence reigned, but it was comfortable.

"Dominic," she said after a moment, her voice barely above a whisper, "I've been thinking."

"About?" I asked, even though part of me knew—could feel the weight of her thoughts like a stone in my gut.

"The wedding." She sat up, turning to face me, her eyes serious in a way that made my heart clench. "I don't want flashy, just something small... just us, and my father, if he'll come."

Her words were a balm and an ache all at once. I understood the unspoken fears behind them—the scars left by a life too familiar with betrayal and loss. She sought simplicity, a shelter from the complexity of our world that had demanded so much from her already.

"Whatever you want, Ivy," I said, my voice rough with emotion. "You know I'd lay the world at your feet if I could."

She nodded, her fingers tracing idle patterns on my chest. In that moment, I was struck by the enormity of her trust, the absolute power she wielded over me without even realizing it.

"Dominic," she murmured, looking up at me, her gaze steady and full of a quiet strength that had nothing to do with the world outside these walls.

I cupped her cheek, the pad of my thumb brushing against her skin. "We can have the world. But I'd give it all up just to have you." And as I spoke those words, I felt their truth resonate deep within my bones. For this woman—in her love, her resilience, her unwavering belief in a man like me—I would forsake everything else. Because she was everything.

Chapter 18
Dominic

I felt a chill slice through the warm evening air as I spotted a figure at the gates of the estate. It was him—her father—standing there like some silent specter from our shared, bloody past. My heart hammering against my ribs, I walked out to meet him, leaving the safety of the grand house behind.

"Mr. Donati," I said, my voice steady despite the turmoil inside.

He didn't bother with words, just nodded, his eyes locking onto mine with a grim sort of resignation. I could read the acceptance in the lines of his face, etched there not by age but by the harsh tutor of loss.

We stood on the gravel path, two men bound by an unspoken understanding. The weight of his gaze was like a physical force, pressing down on me with the gravity of the situation that brought us together under these twisted circumstances.

"You protect her, or I'll bury you," he finally spoke, his voice a low growl of paternal warning.

"Always," I replied without hesitation. In that word was my vow, my future, and the acknowledgment of the threat that lurked in his promise. It was all there, hanging between us—a taut line that neither of us dared to cross.

* * *

I walked out to the cool evening, my heart pounding so loud I could barely hear the rustle of leaves in Dominic's garden. There they were, just standing and staring at each other—Dominic and my father, two forces of nature about to collide.

"Ready?" Dad's voice was gentle as he offered his arm. His eyes held a sadness that made my throat tight and my eyes well up with tears.

"Y-yeah," I stammered, wiping away a tear that escaped. I took his arm, trying to steady myself. It wasn't just walking down an aisle; it felt like walking a tightrope between my past and my future.

The garden was lit by soft golden lights that flickered like many little fireflies. The air smelled of roses and something crisp, like the edge of autumn. I wore a simple ivory gown that flowed around me, making me feel like part of the twilight itself.

Dad led me slowly down the makeshift aisle, his grip on my arm both firm and comforting. The grass whispered under our steps, and the world seemed to hold its breath. All those days of being scared, of feeling trapped, they all led to this moment of fragile beauty.

The whispers of the garden wrapped around us like secrets as we moved closer to where Dominic waited, looking like a statue carved from darkness and power. This was it, the beginning or the end—I wasn't sure which. But ready or not, it was happening.

* * *

I stood before Dominic, the last steps closing the gap between us. His hands reached out, barely trembling, and when they touched mine, it was like a promise all on its own. I had seen those hands command men and shape destinies, yet now they cradled mine with a gentleness that felt like a whispered secret.

"Isabella Ivy Donati," Dominic's voice broke the silence, his eyes never leaving mine, "do you take me to be your wedded husband, to live together in marriage, to love me, comfort me, honor and keep me for better or worse, for richer or poorer, in sickness and health, and forsaking all others, be faithful only to me for as long as we both shall live?"

His vow hung heavy in the air, like it was something solid we could both hold on to. It sounded more like an oath than anything I'd ever heard, spoken by a voice that was used to being obeyed. My heart hammered against my heart, freaking heck, loud enough I thought everyone could hear it.

"I do," I said, my voice a soft echo of his intensity. "And do you, Dominic Mancini, take me to be your wedded wife, to hold from this day forward, for better, for worse, for richer, for poorer, in sickness and in health, to love and to cherish, until death parts us?"

He nodded once, sharply. "I do." The words were a steel trap snapping shut, final and unbreakable.

Then, the moment we had waited for—the kiss. As our lips met, something wild and electric passed between us. It was dangerous, this kiss, full of power and promise. It felt like the first time all over again, igniting every nerve in my body. This wasn't just a seal of our vows; it was an acknowledgment of the storm we were choosing to weather together.

As we parted, I saw the world in a way I never had before—through the eyes of a woman who belonged to a man whose life was a delicate balance of light and darkness. But in that kiss, I knew no matter what came next, we'd face it together.

* * *

The wedding guests had scattered like whispers on the wind, leaving just the echo of their congratulations behind. I watched as my father, a silhouette against the fading light, took firm steps toward Dominic. His eyes were fixed, his jaw set in that way that meant business.

"Dominic," he said, voice low and heavy with an unspoken warning. My heart skipped. He laid a hand on Dominic's shoulder, a grip that was more than just a touch—it was a demand.

"Promise me," my father's words cut through the cool evening air, "you'll keep Ivy away from your darker dealings. She's not made for that life."

I stood a little way off, wrapped in the soft ivory fabric of my dress, the surrounding garden slipping into twilight. They both seemed like statues, two men carved from stone and old-world codes.

Dominic's nod was almost imperceptible. "You have my word," he said, and I could hear the iron will in his voice, the same tone he used when sealing fates within our world.

My father searched his face for a moment longer, then stepped back, satisfied or perhaps resigned. As they separated, a chill ran down my spine. Dominic turned to look at me, his gaze holding mine across the distance. In his eyes, I saw a silent promise echoing his spoken one.

But there was something else, a shadow that flickered behind the certainty—a recognition that some promises were impossible to keep. He knew, as did I, that the darkness had wound its way around my heart, threading through it like the ivy for which I was named. And in that moment, I understood it wasn't something he dragged me into; it was something I walked into with open eyes.

This life, this man, this love—it was all a choice, one I had made knowingly. The darkness was part of me now, chosen and embraced.

Chapter 19

Ivy

I stood by his side, my hand finding its place on the curve of his arm. This wasn't the timid clutch of a secret affair; it was the grip of a woman who knew her power. Dominic's world, our world, watched with eyes sharp as knives.

"Dominic," I said, loud enough for the room to hear, "they need to see us together." My voice didn't wobble. It couldn't afford to.

He nodded once, and the murmur in the room grew into a storm. Faces of stone and eyes like ice turned to appraise me. I felt the weight of their stares, the silent questions they hurled my way. Could this young thing stand with one of their own? Did she have the steel for it?

"Signora," a voice broke through, slick with doubt. Marco, one of the old guard, stepped forward, his lips twisted in a smirk that didn't reach his eyes.

"Marco," I greeted him, steady as the ground beneath us.

"Tell me," he probed, "what makes you think you can survive in our world?" It was a challenge wrapped in a question.

"Because I understand it," I replied, my voice cool as the wine that would later be poured. "Respect is earned, not given freely. And I'm not afraid to earn mine."

There were nods, some grudging, as the crowd took in my words. But I saw it then—the glint in another's eye, that flash of disrespect that couldn't be countered with words alone.

The night had stretched on, tense as a wire about to snap. A figure moved too quickly from shadow to light. My heart kicked up a notch—instinct screamed danger. The sound of a gun being drawn was a whisper but to me, it roared.

Time slowed. I turned, my weapon already in hand, a gift from Dominic that felt like an extension of my will. One shot. The figure crumpled. Silence reigned, then applause like thunder.

"Brava, Signora," someone called out, and the title was a cloak I wrapped around myself. They saw me now, not just as Dominic's, but as someone to respect—or fear.

Dominic's hand found mine, his grip tight. "You did well," he murmured, and I knew he meant every word.

The night carried on, and I stayed by his side, my mind whirling with what I'd done, with what we'd become. We were a unit, bound by blood and ambition. And I wouldn't have it any other way.

***

The night air was thick with the scent of olives and citrus, the estate's gardens transformed into a scene from a fairytale. Twinkling fairy lights wove through the trees like captured stars, casting a soft glow on the faces of our guests. Firelight flickered from torches staked along the paths, creating shadows that danced just as much as we did.

Dominic's hand was firm in mine as we swirled among our allies. His eyes never left my face, a silent message that I had earned my place here in this circle of power. The music was a living thing, wrapping around us, a mix of old-world strings and the heartbeat rhythm of modernity.

In Dominic's arms, I could almost forget the weight of the stares, the whispered bets on my survival in this underworld where the weak were devoured. But I wasn't weak. Not anymore. I moved with him step for step, my body learning the language of his silent cues.

"Trust me," Dominic had said once, and I did, even as I leaned back in his arms, my head grazing his hand, trusting him to hold me steady.

It was then I saw it—the slight shift in a server's eyes, the hesitation before he poured wine into a glass. My heart clenched; something was wrong. I pulled myself upright and excused us with a smile that didn't reach my eyes.

"Excuse us," I murmured, my voice steady despite the alarm ringing in my skull. "We must toast our guests."

Dominic nodded, understanding flashing in his gaze. We approached the table where the wine waited, my mind racing. I reached out, my fingers brushing the bottle, and there it was—a residue, nearly imperceptible. Poison.

"Dominic," I whispered, and handed him the bottle.

His eyes darkened. In one swift movement, he grasped the server by the collar, dragging him into the light. The crowd fell silent, all mirth gone, replaced by a cold fury that settled over the garden like a shroud.

"Who sent you?" Dominic demanded, his voice a low growl that echoed against the stone walls of our home.

The server's eyes darted around, seeking an escape that didn't exist. He knew, as did we all, what came next.

"Blood and fire," Dominic pronounced, his verdict final.

The traitor didn't scream for long as the flames consumed him, a stark reminder of the price of betrayal. I watched, my spine straight, my expression impassive. This was our world—cruel and beautiful, bound by loyalty and fear.

"Let this be a lesson," Dominic declared to the gathered crowd. "Our bond is sacred."

And as the ashes fluttered to the ground, mixing with the earth, I knew they held a warning to any who dared challenge us. For we were united, Dominic and I, guardians of this precarious empire we called home.

***

The ashes still warmed the ground when I felt his eyes on me, searching for a crack in my armor. But there was none to find. I turned to Dominic, our gazes locking in the flickering light.

"We protect this," I said, no louder than a breath, yet with all the steel of the empire we stood upon. "Whatever it takes."

His hand found mine, fingers lacing with a grip that spoke of battles fought and yet to come. The allies watched, their respect hard-earned and their fear just beginning to take root. Dominic's world was mine now, not by chance, but by choice.

The night wore on, the tension slowly giving way to a cautious celebration once more. It wasn't until we retreated to the quiet of our chambers that the façade fell away, revealing the man beneath the don.

"Ivy," he began, a shadow crossing his chiseled features, "I'm scared of what you're becoming."

I studied him then, seeing the lines of worry that marred his brow, the weight he carried for us both. A smile found its way to my lips, not quite sad, not quite joyful.

"Dominic," I replied, tilting my head as if to dismiss his fears, "I'm just becoming yours."

And in those words lay the truth of it—his darkness had become my own, just as my light now threaded through his shadows. We were bound together, not just by a ring or a vow, but by the very essence of who we'd chosen to be.

***

The sheets were cool against our skin as we came together, the rush of the day melting into a slow burn between us. Dominic's touch was a language I'd learned fluently, one that spoke of need entwined with a fierce protectiveness. The city's heartbeat stuttered and slowed outside our window, the night holding its breath in the quiet after the storm.

I lay my head on his chest, feeling the rise and fall with each breath he took. His heart drummed a steady rhythm beneath my cheek, a silent promise that echoed through the stillness of our room. We moved together unhurriedly, every motion a testament to the trust we'd built. The world beyond these walls could wait; here, time belonged only to us.

As we found our release, the tension that had gripped us unwound. Dominic's fingers traced idle patterns on my back, his presence a constant in the fluidity of our connection. The air hummed with an energy spent and yet somehow renewed, wrapping us in a cocoon of our own making.

Later, as the edges of sleep threatened to pull me under, I caught sight of the ring on my finger—a band of silver, simple but heavy with meaning. I twisted it around, the metal catching what little light seeped in from the moonlit curtains. "You still think I'm too innocent?" I whispered into the silence, my voice small but sure.

Dominic shifted and his lips grazed my throat, a sensation that sent a shiver down my spine even now. "No," he growled, his breath warm against my skin. "I think you're lethal."

That word hung in the air, stark and true. Lethal. Not the girl I once was, but the woman I'd become—forged in fire and bound by shadows. Dominic knew it. And somewhere deep inside, where fear tangled with a dark kind of thrill, so did I.

***

The moon had slipped away when I felt his chest rise in a long, deep breath. His arms tightened around me, pulling me closer, as if even in sleep he couldn't bear the thought of distance between us. Sleep clung to my eyelids, but the weight of his words kept me anchored in wakefulness.

I turned in his embrace, facing him. The darkness draped over us like a velvet curtain, yet his features were etched into my mind's eye—sharp, unforgiving, beautiful. Lethal, he'd said. The word echoed in my thoughts, bouncing off the walls of my skull until it settled in my bones.

"Dominic," I murmured, watching for any sign that he was still with me in this quiet hour. His eyes flickered open, two pools of ink reflecting a world I was only beginning to understand.

"Sleep, Ivy," he whispered, his hands tracing the curve of my waist. But sleep wouldn't come, not when the night was so full of whispers and my mind raced with possibilities of what lay ahead.

"Are we safe?" The question slipped out, born from the shadows that played across the room, casting doubt where there had been certainty.

"Always." His answer was a shield, a promise made of steel and blood. Yet I knew that safety was a fragile thing, something that could shatter with the pull of a trigger or the slice of a blade.

"Promise me," I pressed, needing to hear the words despite knowing they were just air, just sound shaped by lips and teeth and tongue.

"I promise, Ivy. No one will hurt you." He sounded sure, resolute, the don of our silent kingdom promising protection from threats seen and unseen.

"Because of you," I said softly, not a question but an acknowledgment of the power he wielded.

"Because of us," he corrected, and there was pride in his voice, a fierce joy that we were bound together in this dangerous dance.

"Us," I repeated, letting the word fill me up, a mantra against the dark. His hand found mine, fingers interlacing, a tangible symbol of unity. With his touch, the city's silence outside didn't feel so pressing, the night not so impenetrable.

"Go to sleep," he urged again, but as I closed my eyes, I knew that rest would be fitful. Dreams of blood and fire awaited me, a testament to the life I now shared with Dominic. And when dawn broke, bringing light to dispel the shadows, we would face whatever came together.

Chapter 20

Ivy

Months had bled into one another, seamless and relentless. I stood beside Dominic, my hands deep in the clandestine workings of our empire. Together, we were a storm no one dared to weather—our names whispered with a mixture of reverence and fear. I had learned the language of power well, fluent in its harsh cadences and chilling silences.

The business had become part of me, its pulse throbbing in my veins as I ordered hits and negotiated terms with a cold precision that would have been foreign to the girl I once was. Dominic, with his dark eyes always watching, seemed pleased with the metamorphosis. He never said it, but I felt it in the way he deferred to my judgment, in the silent nod that followed my decisions.

It had been too long since we visited my father. The man who had once been larger than life now seemed diminished, an echo of the titan he'd been. His house smelt of time and decaying memories, a stark contrast to the sterile luxury of our own home. When we arrived, he looked at us, his gaze lingering on Dominic with a wariness sharpened by age.

"Hello father," I said softly, stepping into the embrace of a man who suddenly seemed so small. His arms clung to me with a desperation that clawed at my heart. I could feel the tremors running through him, the unspoken pleas for forgiveness—or perhaps just understanding. He pulled back, staring into my face like he was committing it to memory, his fingers brushing my hair back like he used to when I was a child.

"Look at you, Ivy," he murmured, his voice raspy with disuse. "You've grown so strong."

There was pride there, but also something else—a shadow of remorse that made me want to reassure him, to lie and say that everything was alright. But we both knew better. We both understood the sacrifices that had been made, the lines that had been crossed. We existed in a world where love was a vulnerability, but just once, I felt it wholly.

"Thanks, Dad," I replied, forcing a smile that felt as heavy as the gun strapped to my thigh.

He nodded, glancing over at Dominic who stood a respectful distance away, the ever-watchful sentinel. There was a silent exchange between them, an acknowledgment of the roles they played in my life. My father's grip tightened briefly before he let go, stepping back into the role of the observer, leaving Dominic and me to navigate the dangerous waters we called home.

As we left my father's house, I couldn't shake the feeling of transience that clung to the walls, the sense that everything we knew could crumble with a word, a bullet, a betrayal. Yet, as Dominic's hand found mine, the solid warmth of his fingers entwined with mine offered a silent promise—a conviction that together, we were invincible.

***

The air was thick with the scent of aged leather and the subtle scent of gunmetal as I sat at the long mahogany table that had become my command center. A shaft of moonlight crept through the blinds, casting a silver glow over the papers and photographs spread out before me. The glint of Dominic's watch caught my eye as he approached, his movements as silent as the promises we kept.

He slid a small velvet box across the table toward me. Its sudden appearance amidst maps marked with territories and reports of skirmishes felt like an intrusion from another life. My fingers brushed the soft fabric, hesitating for a heartbeat before opening it. Inside lay a necklace, the chain delicate and the pendant emblazoned with a crest I knew well—the symbol of Dominic's family.

"This was my mother's," he said, his voice a low rumble that reverberated in the hollows of the quiet room. "Now it's yours."

I lifted the necklace from its resting place, the metal cool against my skin. It was more than a piece of jewelry; it was a declaration. With this act, he tied me to his history, to the bloodline of his power. I thought of my father, how his embrace lingered as if trying to shield me one last time. There was no shielding here, only the stark reality of what we'd become.

"Trouble on the West Coast," one of Dominic's men interrupted from the doorway, a loyal shadow among many. His eyes darted to the necklace briefly before meeting mine, respect etched into the lines of his face.

Dominic's gaze didn't waver from mine as he addressed the messenger. "We don't move until she says so."

The weight of command settled on my shoulders, but it wasn't heavy—it was a mantle I'd grown accustomed to wearing. I raised an eyebrow, relishing the cool draft of certainty that whispered through the room. "We move at dawn."

Orders would be given, plans drawn up, and our will imposed. The forced proximity of these walls became the crucible where my youth was smelted into iron resolve. Where once I may have hesitated, now there was only the thrill of dominion and the cold clarity of purpose.

As I clasped the necklace around my throat, the pendant rested against my pulse—a constant reminder that my heart now beat to the rhythm of a dark empire, alongside a man who traded whispers with shadows and turned violence into verse.

***

I stood in the center of Dominic's office, a place that once felt more like a lion's den than a sanctuary. The men encircled me, their faces carved from years of obedience and violence, yet here they were, hanging on my every word. My commands sliced through the thick air, clear and I must admit, decisive, "Reroute the shipments to avoid the checkpoints. Double the watch on our territories. I want updates every hour."

They nodded, a sea of stoic masks, but their eyes betrayed them—flashes of admiration, maybe even fear. I wasn't just the girl who'd been caught in Dominic's gravity anymore. I was the force that kept his world spinning, the queen in this dark game of chess.

"Anything else?" Marco, one capo, asked, his voice rough like gravel.

"Tell the men on the ground to keep it clean. We can't afford mistakes, not now."

"Understood." He turned on his heel, leaving me with the echo of power resonating in the room.

Later, as the night swallowed the last sliver of daylight, Dominic led me to the rooftop. A table set for two awaited us, champagne glistening under the stars. The city stretched out below, a tapestry of light and shadow, each flickering bulb a story, a life, a secret.

He poured the champagne, its pop a soft exclamation mark in the hush between us. As we clinked glasses, the crystal sang, a delicate chime that seemed too pure for the likes of us.

"Before you..." Dominic started, his voice trailing off as he stared at the skyline. "I never believed in peace. It was a fairy tale, a lie told to pacify children."

I sipped the champagne, the bubbles dancing on my tongue bittersweet. His hand found mine, strong and sure, pulling me closer.

"Then you stormed into my life, a tempest wrapped in silk, and I…" He hesitated, searching for words that usually bent to his will. "You taught me that peace isn't a fairy tale. It's something you build, something you fight for, something worth believing in."

My heart thrummed against the family crest that now lay over it, a symbol of loyalty and legacy. We stood there, king and queen of a kingdom no one else would ever understand, a world built on blood and ambition.

"Here's to peace then," I said, lifting my glass higher.

"To peace," he echoed, the ghost of a smile playing on his lips, and we drank to the future, whatever it might hold.

***

The city's glow cast a halo around us, the night air cool against our skin. I leaned back into Dominic's embrace, his arms a fortress I didn't know I'd ever find comfort in. The champagne had left a trail of warmth down my throat, its sweetness a stark contrast to the night's ambiance—full of sharp edges and whispered promises.

I let a hand drift down, resting it gently over my stomach. Beneath the fabric of my dress, life stirred—a secret kept close, not ready to be shared. Not tonight. Tonight was for other truths, ones we could taste on each other's lips and read in the lines we carved into the world.

Dominic's breath was slow against my ear, matching the rhythm of the city below us. This empire of ours wasn't supposed to know peace, but together we'd wrestled it into submission.

Underneath my palm, I felt the flutter of something new, a tiny heartbeat that beat out a future full of possibilities we both had snatched from the jaws of fate.

"Are you alright?" His voice was soft, concern threading through the two words like silk.

"Better than alright," I answered, my smile hidden in the shadows. This joy was mine to savor alone, just for a little while longer.

The moment stretched out, filled with the silent strength of our bond. As I turned within his grasp, the city lights caught the glint of the ring on my finger—a symbol of power, a tie that bound me to Dominic and this twisted legacy we were entwined with. My eyes held his, sharp as the blade I knew how to wield so well. No longer the girl he'd taken under his dark wing, but a queen—an equal in the kingdom we ruled.

"Come inside," I whispered, feeling the weight of the evening settle around us. "There's still work to be done."

He nodded, the king to my queen, and together we stepped back from the edge, the city sprawling beneath us—a playground for our ambitions, a testament to the blood, fire, and forbidden love that had forged our reign.

Epilogue

Ivy

The early morning rays painted the opulent chamber golden, but it was Dominic's steady warmth beside me that filled me with an overwhelming sense of peace. I shifted slightly, careful not to disturb him, taking in the rise and fall of his chest as he slept on. He looked serene — a stark contrast to the relentless, calculating man who commanded respect in a world shrouded in shadows and danger.

I barely recognized the girl who had once trembled at the sight of him. Now, here I lay, enveloped in the safety of his embrace, reflecting on the twisted path that had brought us together. Fear had turned to fascination, then to something deeper — a connection forged in fire, tested by trials, yet unbreakable in its intensity.

Dominic stirred beside me, his dark lashes fluttering against the high planes of his cheekbones. The furrow between his brows, usually set in a frown when he faced the outside world, relaxed in slumber. A soft smile curled my lips as I reached out, brushing a rogue strand of hair from his forehead with a feather-light touch.

"Morning," I murmured, my voice barely above a whisper, not wanting to chase away the tranquility of dawn just yet.

He opened his eyes, locking onto mine with that piercing gaze that could cut through lies and pretense. There was no need for such defenses here, between us, in the quiet sanctity of our shared space. "Ivy," he said, his voice rough with sleep, yet laced with the underlying strength that defined him.

"Did you sleep well?" I asked, my fingers tracing the outline of the ink that marked his skin, each tattoo a story, a memory etched into flesh.

"Better than I have in years," he replied, drawing me closer until there was no space left between us. His lips met mine in a lingering kiss, not one of possession or fiery passion, but a promise of eternity in its gentle insistence.

In that moment, as the world outside our door continued its restless churn, we existed in a pocket of stillness, a testament to the improbable love that bound a fierce mafia lord to the girl who'd dared to unravel his heart.

* * *

I stepped out of the comfort of our bed, the chill of the morning air a stark contrast to the lingering warmth of Dominic's embrace. He followed suit, rising with a fluidity that spoke of his quiet power. We navigated the space of our shared closet with an ease born of countless mornings just like this one. I selected a soft sweater and skirt, while he chose a crisp shirt, the fabric conforming to his broad shoulders as if it were made for him alone.

"Your tie," I said, my fingers deftly selecting the silk length that matched his eyes. I held it out to him, and with a nod, he approached, allowing me to loop it around his neck. There was a grace in the way we moved together, a silent dance refined by time and intimacy. Each fold, each tuck was a word in our private language, and with a last tug, the knot lay perfect against his collar.

The clink of ceramic and the rich aroma of coffee drew us to the sunlit kitchen where a breakfast for two awaited. He pulled out a chair for me, always the gentleman despite the darkness of his world. I settled into my seat, the table between us no barrier to the connection that hummed in the air.

"Plans for today?" I asked, spooning a dollop of jam onto my toast. The sunlight caught in his hair, turning it to threads of gold, and my heart skipped at the sight.

"Meetings until the afternoon," he replied, his gaze never leaving mine as he bit into a slice of fruit. "But I'll be back before dinner."

"Good," I said, reaching for his hand across the table. "I'll be going over the accounts, making sure everything is as it should be." My role in his empire might be quieter, but it was no less vital. He squeezed my hand in silent thanks, appreciation glowing in his eyes.

"Without you," he began, as he sipped his coffee, "none of this would work. You know that, don't you?"

I felt the weight of his words, heavy with truth and trust. "I do," I responded, the pride in his voice wrapping around me like a warm shawl. Our dreams, once whispered in the dark, now lay open in the morning light—two halves of a whole, striving towards a future forged from love and iron will.

"Then it's another day we conquer together," he said with a smile that promised victories both in boardrooms and in the quiet spaces of our hearts.

"Together," I echoed, the word tasting of hope and the sweet life we'd claimed against all odds.

***

We walked, fingers entwined, through the sprawling estate that was as much a fortress as it was our home. The morning light cast long shadows over manicured lawns, and roses bloomed with such vitality they seemed to compete with the sun itself. Marble statues of ancient gods stood watch, their stone eyes following us with silent approval.

As we passed, staff nodded with practiced deference. The gardener tipped his hat, his hands pausing in their dance with the shears.

A maid, her apron crisp and white, offered a curtsy, her gaze flickering between Dominic and me before returning to her work with a quiet efficiency. Each greeting was a thread in the tapestry of our lives, woven tight with respect and fear.

"Mr. Mancini," one guard ventured, his voice a low rumble as he fell into step just behind us. He was a mountain of a man, suited not for the daylight but for the shadows where our true business lay. "The new security protocols are in place."

"Show them to Ivy later," Dominic ordered without breaking stride. His grip on my hand tightened, a silent message that he trusted me with the bones of our empire.

"Of course, sir," the guard replied, already fading back into his watchful silence.

We continued on, every footstep a claim to the power we held. The estate was more than marble and gardens; it was a symbol of everything we'd built—a kingdom standing strong against those who dared to challenge us.

Dominic led me into his study, a room of dark wood and secrets. He closed the door, and it was as if we left the world outside. Here, in this space, scented with leather and ambition, we shed our titles and became simply two souls bound by a love that had weathered storms.

He pulled out a bottle of aged whiskey, the liquid amber like the eyes that now watched me. "We did it, Ivy," he said, pouring two glasses. "The merger went through without a hitch." His voice thrummed with pride.

"Your vision," I started, accepting the glass he offered. "It's coming to life."

"Ours," he corrected gently. "Without your finesse, the books would never balance."

"To us, then," I toasted, the clink of glass echoing off the walls.

"Us." He echoed, and the word filled the room like a vow. We drank, the heat of the whiskey a slow fire that mirrored the burn in my chest for this man, this life.

"Tell me," he said, setting down his glass and leaning forward, elbows on his desk. "What dreams have you been hiding up your sleeve?"

I hesitated, the rawness of hope making my words tremble. "I've been thinking about a charity. For kids who... who need an out, like I did."

"Then consider it done." Determination lined his face. "We'll build something that lasts, Ivy. Something good from all this darkness."

"Can we really do that?" The question slipped out, heavy with the weight of our past.

"Look at what we've achieved together," he coaxed, his gaze holding mine. "There's nothing we can't do, as long as we stand side by side."

And in that moment, surrounded by books, and the ghosts of decisions made, I believed him. Because with Dominic, the impossible became just another challenge to face together. With him, every heartache and victory was shared, each one forging the bond between us into something unbreakable.

***

I sat beneath the old oak, the leaves whispering secrets as the evening sun dipped low. Dominic was a silent strength beside me, his presence a comforting weight in this world we'd carved out of chaos. The surrounding garden bloomed with life—reds and purples vying for attention against the lush green backdrop.

"Look at us," I murmured, reaching for his hand, feeling the callouses that spoke of hard work and harder choices. "Did you ever think we'd find peace like this?"

He wrapped his hands around mine, the warmth there seeping into my bones. "With you, Ivy, I believed we could find anything," he said, his voice carrying the depth of oceans. "You're my compass—the true north I never knew I needed."

I leaned into him, letting my gratitude for our love spill over. "Thank you, for this life. For the love that defies all odds."

"Always," he whispered back, sealing it with a kiss that tasted of promises kept.

We spent the rest of the afternoon preparations, laughter and anticipation filling the air. Our steps were in sync as we set the table, checked the silverware, and arranged fresh flowers—a dance we both knew well.

"Perfect," I said, surveying our handiwork, the table aglow with candles flickering like little beacons of welcome.

"Like the hosts," He teased, pulling me close for a quick spin, laughter bubbling up between us.

The gathering unfolded like a scene from a dream. Friends and allies filled the rooms, their voices a symphony of camaraderie. We navigated conversations, ensuring glasses remained full and smiles stayed wide. When we spoke, others listened—a subtle nod to the unspoken power we wielded together.

"Dominic, Ivy, you two are a force," Marco, raised his glass in salute.

"Together, we are unstoppable," Dominic replied, his arm finding its way around my waist.

As the evening wore on, the crowd thinned until only the night's quiet lingered. We slipped away, our footsteps echoing softly on the marble floor.

"Today was a success," I said, leaning my head against his shoulder.

"Every day with you is." His voice was soft but sure, the certainty in his words wrapping around me like a blanket.

We got to our bedroom, the sanctuary where all our masks could fall away. He kissed me then, a kiss that spoke of endless tomorrows and the love that had become the bedrock of our lives.

"Goodnight, my Ivy," he said as we lay together, the darkness wrapping around us, a cocoon spun from silk and shadows.

"Goodnight, Dominic." In his embrace, I found the tranquility and fulfillment that came from knowing we had built a thriving love that would stand the test of time. And as we drifted off to sleep, I held onto the feeling that, together, we were home.

[Love dark mafia romance Dark Arranged Brides By Ana Slash!](#)

Favorite series

[Billionaire Older man younger woman seriesby Anastasia Salsh](#)

Printed in Dunstable, United Kingdom